ASKO SAHLBERG

TRANSLATED FROM THE FINNISH
BY EMILY JEREMIAH
AND FLEUR JEREMIAH

Peirene

He

AUTHOR

Asko Sahlberg, born in 1964, has acquired a fame in Finland that has yet to be replicated in the English-speaking world. He published his first novel in 2000 and has written steadily since then, completing his ninth work, *The Brothers*, in 2010.

TRANSLATORS

Emily Jeremiah and Fleur Jeremiah unite as a multi-lingual mother-and-daughter translation team. Emily has an MA in Creative Writing and a PhD in German Studies. Fleur, her mother, is Finnish and has translated both fiction and non-fiction for many years. Emily and Fleur have together produced translations of poems by Helvi Juvonen and Sirkka Turkka.

MEIKE ZIERVOGEL
PEIRENE PRESS

This is a historical novel in miniature form. It deals in dark passions and delivers as many twists as a 500-page epic. And as if that were not enough, each character speaks in a distinct voice. I'm thrilled to publish a book that is as Finnish as a forest in winter but that resembles a work from the American South: William Faulkner's *As I Lay Dying*.

First published in Great Britain in 2011 by
Peirene Press Ltd
17 Cheverton Road
London N19 3BB
www.peirenepress.com

First published under the original Finnish title *He*
by Werner Söderström Ltd (WSOY)
Copyright © Asko Sahlberg and
Werner Söderström Ltd, 2010, Helsinki, Finland

This translation © Emily Jeremiah and Fleur Jeremiah, 2011

This work has been published with the financial assistance of
FILI – Finnish Literature Exchange

ISBN 978-0-9562840-6-8

Designed by Sacha Davison Lunt
Typeset by Tetragon
Photographic image: Mitsushi Okada/amana images/Getty Images
Printed and bound by T J International, Padstow, Cornwall
Supported by

LOTTERY FUNDED

Peirene

ASKO SAHLBERG

*TRANSLATED FROM THE FINNISH
BY EMILY JEREMIAH
AND FLEUR JEREMIAH*

The
Brothers

THE FARMHAND

I have barely caught the crunch of snow and I know who is coming. Henrik treads heavily and unhurriedly, as is his wont, grinding his feet into the earth. The brothers are so different. Erik walks fast, with light steps; he is always in a hurry, here then gone.

The steps pass my cabin and cease. I stand up, go to the door, push it cautiously open. Henrik stands tree-like in the middle of the yard. He takes his time, stares at the house. The windows glimmer with light, muffled by the thick curtains. The house looks bigger than it really is, silhouetted against the forest, magnified by the dark. He knows its precise size, of course, and how much grief and disappointment it holds.

If I were in Henrik's shoes, I would not wish to go in, either; I would not dare. Mind you, hasn't he been given more courage than is good for a man? He has never been able to control himself, not since he was a child. He is like a crazy horse that needs reining in. But even the most reckless of men will not do some things unless forced, not if the time is not right. Or only if they are cursed with extreme stupidity. But Henrik is no fool. On the move again, he heads for the stable.

I sit here, breathing fast. The wind pokes the cabin walls. My nose tells me the fire is dying. My eyes see nothing, for they have spied another kind of dark.

The war has been waged, but here we may yet have corpses.

ANNA

Yesterday I saw the footprints of a wolf at the edge of the snowy field. That was how I guessed. That was why I went outside, into the pale dawn. I went silently, as if non-existent. I smelt the night and the cold tree trunks. I saw my breath steaming in the frosty air. I did not need to find the boot-prints in the yard but I still looked for them. I avoided staring at them so that I would not run off. I did not look in the direction of the stable, though my back strained to twist free from its base.

I would have returned inside had I not spotted the Farmhand. He was standing in front of his cabin, immobile and eternal, grown from the soil. He is a mystery. He is always there, and yet he is not. You see in him many generations of men with gnarled fists and bony knees. Such men are generally either coming from the forest or going to the forest. Or else they are harrowing a field or sitting on some steps, smoking a pipe without moving their lips. There is no point wondering what the Old Mistress sees in the Farmhand. We all pretend we do not hear the hem of her faded muslin skirt brushing the path across the yard at night.

And then an owl always cries.

The Farmhand was watching me. I could tell because he had turned his head. The hollowed-out footprints from the road to the yard led back to him. In these parts, all prints lead to him. Everything originates from him, more or less, although he does not know it. He is the only one of us who is free from the sin of lying and thus he is innocent.

I finally reached the steps and re-entered the house. And then I just existed. The day had arrived in full, and now I listen to the Old Mistress moving about upstairs, stiff-hipped. I know that the maid has been to her room, that the heavy curtains have been opened and the bed has been made. The room smells of powder, bad temper and the scent Erik says costs too much. On the wall hangs the only painting in the house. It shows a man with bushy eyebrows. He stares at you from underneath his stiff-brimmed hat, which does not fit him at all and appears to have grown directly from his skull, extending out from his forehead and above his ears like two horns fused together. Maybe the Old Mistress pauses to stare back at those eyes, painted near-black. For a moment, she sits down in her chair, upholstered in worn brocade, but soon restlessness forces her back on her feet. Her unease disappears later in the afternoon and mellows into empty-faced lassitude in the course of the evening.

From outside, I can hear the sound of sharp blows. The Farmhand is chopping wood. His axe strikes rhythmically; he has an internal clock, its tempo beats in his arms.

I have an internal clock, too. It has stopped at the early hours of the morning.

A shadow flits across the window. I go to see: Henrik is moving slowly towards the woodshed. He is as broad-shouldered as ever, but is he still the same? Immediately, my back tenses like a spring. I am all fluttery as I hurry into the hall and push my feet into shoes. I slip out on to the steps. I am so light that the snow, trampled hard, does not betray my movements. I turn off the pathway and reach a place behind the cowshed where I can listen. I hold my breath, to hear without being heard.

'At least the place hasn't been left to rot,' says Henrik. 'I could see that when I arrived last night. The moon's as bright as the sun sometimes.'

It takes a while for the Farmhand to answer. 'Bright enough to do battle by?'

'We didn't do much battle at night. Only a couple of times. We were near here one night, over by the village.'

The Farmhand's axe is still. 'I heard. You burnt down the houses.'

'What does it matter who did the burning? I saw to it this house wasn't burnt. Though the enemy had a friend here, so they said.'

The Farmhand spits. He barely makes a noise. 'Depends how you see it. Some had a different enemy – that goes for many men we know.'

'Well, now we have an emperor. New regime. It's time to put away the weapons and start thinking about the future.' I can picture Henrik's face, set, like a pale piece of wood resting between his shoulders. 'Things will get better, believe me.'

'It's not about believing. Nothing'll change if you swap one master for another.'

'I wouldn't put it quite like that. But there'll be time to talk about it. I should go and greet Mother and whoever else is in there now.'

'Erik went to town yesterday, with Mauri. And the Old Mistress hasn't been too well lately.'

Henrik does not sound surprised, or even anxious. He asks in an expressionless voice, 'What's wrong with Mother, then?'

'Maybe I shouldn't say.'

'Of course you should. Out with it.'

I can tell the Farmhand isn't looking at Henrik. 'Maybe it pains a mother to see her sons fight each other.'

'My fight was with the King. There's a big difference.'

'Maybe.'

A crow caws in the pine trees. Wind blows over the cowshed roof. Henrik says, 'At least the place looks in good condition.'

I sense he is about to leave even before he turns on his heel.

The Farmhand grunts and carries on chopping firewood as if he had never lost his earlier rhythm – rather like sounds deep inside a forest are briefly drowned out by a gust of wind, before returning. He groans, but not because of the physical exertion.

I wait with my back pressed against the wall until the sound of Henrik's steps has died away. I creep to the corner of the cowshed just in time to see the wiry figure disappear through the door. I stand still, with a throbbing in my throat that is rooted in my heart.

THE OLD MISTRESS
The hens are laying well. I was wise enough to pay for a good breed. I should teach the new girl to bake.

HENRIK
She has definitely not changed for the better. I said it upon leaving and I will say it again: a cow that no longer yields milk should be taken to the knacker's yard. Never mind honouring your mother, I might as well pay my respects to the whore of Babylon.

She stands with her back to me, merely to make a point. She fiddles with her hair, which already shows some grey. But I can see her neck trembling. The grandfather clock strikes in the corner and the new housemaid clatters about in the kitchen. The girl still has a lot to learn. Or is it too much to ask that servants do their job without creating a din worthy of the Old Testament? That is what is wrong with these people. They are useless and lazy. They are bringing this country to ruin. I had to travel hundreds of versts to get here, only to hate my homeland all over again. In St Petersburg, I thought I could strip off this nation like a torn shirt, but it was not that easy. I bear the mark of Cain. It is not enough of a destiny for a man to be born at the wrong time, he also has to be born in the wrong place. And what's more, he has no stake in that place whatsoever.

Mother turns suddenly, as if spun round by a gust of wind. Her face looks pale in the slanting light. The wrinkles that begin at the corners of her eyes and the sides of her nose have deepened, and the skin under her chin has loosened. 'What sort of a place is it, then?' she asks.

'There's no other city like it,' I reply. 'There are more fountains there than there are houses in Turku, and Nevsky Prospect is so packed with carriages you can scarcely squeeze between them. There's progress, well-being, plenty of rich folk. Not even Stockholm can compete.'

Her eyelids don't flicker. 'If it's so grand there, wouldn't you have been better off staying?'

I will not lose my temper; I will not give her the satisfaction. I answer, 'Yes, of course, but history's being made. Good men are needed here, now that we're lucky enough to be part of the Empire.'

'Lucky, you say?'

'Call it luck, or else the Emperor doing us a favour out of the goodness of his heart. Of course, many of the local peasants haven't yet grasped this.'

'But you were right to return to the peasants?'

'I've already said so.'

She turns her back on me again. I move to the table. I draw a line in the dust shrouding it. Has the new maid been engaged only to receive free board? Mother begins nervously fingering those foolish porcelain knick-knacks collected on top of the chest of drawers: angels and horses and sheep and unicorns. Grotesque reminders of her urban childhood, long since lost. Though there is still something childlike about her, always will be. I would bet my boots she is itching to grab that bottle on the side table. So I go and pour myself a drink.

'I hear Erik is in Vaasa with Mauri,' I say. 'The Farmhand told me.'

Her voice couldn't get any more tense. 'They seem to have more than enough business over there. But what do I know? It could be something really important. I made up my mind a long time ago that I don't need to bother with the affairs of this house any more. Erik deals with all that. And I think I've earned a quiet life by now.'

'Yes, for sure. And Erik has...'

'A capable wife to support him? Is that what you were going to say?'

'Capable, why not? Not a bad expression.'

She half-turns towards me. 'Why did you come back?' She seems to direct the question to a third person, hidden from view.

'What sort of a question is that? Surely a man can come home.'

'Home? No use trying to pull the wool over my eyes. I know full well there's no such thing as home where you're concerned.'

Strange, how at times the easiness of words can make your whole face feel light. 'A man can't always fathom his comings and goings. I felt there was unfinished business.'

'Business?'

'Yes. Certain business.'

She snorts, weakly but furiously. 'It'd be better if you saw to your certain business elsewhere.'

'But I happen to be here. So, not much you can do about it.'

I am about to step into the doorway when she says, 'You obviously didn't do that well in St Petersburg.'

I stop. I ask over my shoulder, 'Why d'you say that?'

'There's not one new horse in the stable.'

She got that off her chest. Indeed she did, but let her have that small consolation in all its pettiness. I enter the hall and my gaze collides with the Farmhand. He is hanging around next to the wall as if it were his job. This little act gets him a real house. If there were any justice in the world, he would be living in a hole in the ground with smoke vents, and spend his days burrowing away deep down in the earth. I

stare at him for a while before I snarl, 'Why are you
skulking here?'

'You can say what you like,' he says in his irritatingly
slow way. 'But I've never been caught skulking.'

'Anyone'd think you were standing there with your
ears pricked up, listening to other people's talk.'

He bares his blackened gums. 'Not possible. I've
been deaf at least since you were fresh out of swaddling
clothes.'

'In other words, you've been deaf for a long time.'

'Or maybe I can still hear perfectly well.'

He should be flogged. He has the nerve to stand
there in front of me with his hat on. The Devil knows
why everyone here esteems him so. What strings did he
pull in his day? That must all have happened before my
time and then been handed on, just like the bad blood
they say one generation passes to the next. Thank
God the Farmhand's blood has been stopped up. Then
again, he could have a brother he has kept quiet about,
maybe even a whole brood of uncouth men, fellows
who stand around in dirty boots on rugs bought by
others in Vaasa, lacking the manners to remove their
smelly, ragged hats.

I glare at him until he finally turns and hobbles
outside. I'm tempted to speed him up with a kick. They
say sons inherit the sins of their fathers. My father's sin
was taking that shameless rat into this house, leaving
me to shoulder the burden.

Mother has obviously been listening, for she slams
the drawing-room door shut behind my back.

Just then, I hear a rustle in the passage leading towards the kitchen. Are there ears in every nook and cranny of this madhouse? I stride in the direction of the sound, squeeze into a dark corner and freeze. I sense it: the scent. What an irony, for a man to experience all the smells of a world metropolis only for his feet to be nailed to the floor by a faint scent that brings him slap-bang face to face with the past.

THE FARMHAND

It has always been the way round here: you say something when you mean something completely different, or at least more. There would have been no point continuing my squabble with Henrik. I might as well talk to a barn wall, with the barn about to fall on top of me.

So I went out again. I felt the frost sharpening. The coldest winter months are lying in wait. I had to go to the forest. On a good day, you can hear nothing there but your own thoughts. I could have inspected the traps, and I started off in the right direction, but a strange weariness forced me to sit down on a tree stump. As I sat, I tried not to think of Henrik, and so I thought of him.

Anyone can see he has been to war. That sort of thing is etched on a man's face, like exhaustion or grief, but I saw more in him: I saw what he used to be. A human being never sheds his past. He drags it around like an old overcoat and you know him by this coat, by the way it looks and smells. Henrik's coat is heavy and gloomy, exuding the dark stench of blood.

It all began with the horse. So little is needed for a man's life to go wrong. At first the horse was a colt. This colt lived on the neighbouring farm. The day Henrik laid eyes on the colt, and saw the horse it would become, the fate of this house was determined. Henrik was born to understand horses. In any other man, such an understanding would be a gift. In Henrik's case, the gift proved a curse. He didn't see in the colt a future work-horse or even a mount. Such a vision was not enough for Henrik. Was he looking for something in animals that he did not dare look for in humans? I was sharpening my scythe at the edge of the field when I heard Henrik's breathless voice behind my shoulder: 'I'm going to get a horse.'

I smiled. One underestimates one's own bygone dreams, sneers at them as they were sneered at in their day by obtuse old men. I asked anyway, 'Where will you get one of those? There's many a grown man doesn't manage it.'

'From Jansson's farm,' Henrik said. 'And it isn't a horse yet, it's only a colt. But I'll work enough days for Jansson for it to be mine when it's grown up.'

'How can you work for Jansson? You're not a tenant of his.'

Had I been more alert, I would have heard the determination in Henrik's voice. 'I'll do it anyway. I'll work for Jansson as long as it takes to get the horse. It'll be a big stallion.'

'Can't it be bought? You should at least ask your father.'

'It wouldn't be mine if Father bought it. I'll earn it myself.'

'Well, in that case, it'll be a man's horse, not a boy's.'

I did not even notice that Henrik raised his head too proudly for a boy his age. 'I'm almost a man now.'

'Or you became a man when you decided to earn that horse.'

A man's life, looked back on, often makes him clutch at his heart. If I could return to the moment when the half-grown Henrik told me about the horse, I would throw the scythe down onto the field. I would grab the boy by the scruff of his neck and alter the future. Horse deals are not the business of a youth who has not yet even earned his first pair of boots. And there was enough work at home for a small army. However, I was not the master of the house, only a servant. And servants do not, as a rule, meddle in their masters' affairs.

So Henrik began doing jobs for Jansson. On Sundays and long weekday evenings he repaired Jansson's barns and built versts of fencing round fields. He would only turn up at home after sunset, blank-eyed with exhaustion, like a spectre. For his age, he was tall and frighteningly strong, even before he began hammering fence posts into the ground and lifting stones out of their way. After five years, he had become a man and the colt had become a horse. In a way, they grew up together, unaware of each other, or maybe, on the contrary, too aware of each other, united by some mysterious bond. You never know with animals like Henrik and the horse.

Finally, I too saw the horse. We had threshed the grain and I had promised to help out Jansson. His labourer had stepped on a nail and was suffering from blood poisoning. At first, I did not give the matter any thought, it had slipped my mind, but then I walked past Jansson's enclosure and noticed something standing there, something that was too big to stand there – unless the enclosure had shrunk.

I saw at once that the animal would be no use to anyone. It would probably kill a man one day, unless somebody had the wits to put it down before that happened. Its size was unnatural; it was not fat, but excessively muscular. It was not just one horse but one and a half, or at least one and a third. Its hooves were like buckets that had got stuck on its feet, coming back from the well. But it was its gaze that sent a shiver down my spine. Over the years, as he wanders through life, a man gets used to the gentle eyes of horses. But Henrik's horse had the burning eyes of a wolf or a lion, or maybe the Beast of the Book of Revelation.

I had never made the acquaintance of an animal with such a severe stare.

'So you decided to give a monster like that to a young man,' I said to Jansson.

He pushed his hat to the back of his head and sighed. 'I didn't want to. But the boy wouldn't stop pleading. And it might yet become useful.'

'It'll never be an Officer of the Guard's parade horse, that's for sure. Has it ever pulled a plough?'

He sighed again. Or was he panting out of sheer terror? 'We gave it a try, but it's just too unruly.'

'And you'll attend Henrik's funeral with a good conscience?'

He shoved his hat over his eyes, probably to avoid seeing the creature glaring at us from the enclosure. 'Well, there's not a lot I can do about it now.'

There would be no funeral. This became clear to me as I was weeding the ditch between our and Jansson's lands and saw Henrik, speeding along on the horse as if he had been born to ride it. I do not know which one of them spotted me, but in any case they started storming towards me. I stared as they approached. I heard the thudding of the heavy hooves and the low whinnying of the horse. I decided – if I was able to decide anything, in my fright – that as I would not have time to run to the edge of the forest, it would be best to throw myself face-down into the ditch. I was on the point of doing so when the horse came abruptly to a halt. It did not seem to stop, in fact; instead it just ceased moving instantaneously. It floated in the air for a moment with its front hooves raised. Then it stood there as if it were already bored.

'So is it yours now?' I asked.

Henrik did not look like a rider on horseback, but like someone or something that had pushed out its head and shoulders, and finally the rest of its body, through the skin on the horse's back. He replied,

'It's not yet mine. But next week the five years will be up.'

'So they will be. Jansson's already letting you ride it, I see.'

'Jansson's in town.'

'And you took the horse. You couldn't wait till next week.'

'I didn't take it. I'll return it to the stable soon.'

Just then, I caught the smell of the horse. It reminded me of a graveyard in autumn. 'You'd better. I expect it's got a name by now. I hope it's a name fit for an elephant.'

'It's called Horse.'

'Even Jansson wouldn't give a stallion such a stupid name.'

Maybe Henrik's hatred of me was born at that moment. 'It's called Horse!'

I would have said something conciliatory but I did not have the chance. As unexpectedly as it had stopped, the horse turned, or rather it did a furious backward roll in the air. Faster than I could have said 'Amen', they were racing ahead, already in the middle of the meadow. The smell of the horse still shimmered around me. It was not the smell of others of its kind; it was more pungent and more ominous. Once it had got into your nose, it would not leave. I had to wait another few years before I understood that the beast smelt of war.

THE OLD MISTRESS

Nowadays, a woman's honour is neither here nor there, if it ever was. When there are no men of honour, there can be no women of honour. Men charge round in a woman's life like mad bulls, and the wisest thing to do would be to sit quietly in a dimly lit corner. But what can you do when there is blood in your veins? That blood will surge and make its demands. And then you have a thirst that is not quenched by drinking.

ANNA

I hear him through the walls. The walls breathe fear and shame into me. My hands are stuck in dough, forgotten, turned to stone. The Old Mistress will arrive soon and begin nagging, but she should not blame me. I did not want a maid who cannot even bake. Erik suggested we get the new girl from town, but the Old Mistress had gone and made a promise to the tailor's widow and there was nothing to be done about it.

I would prefer to be frightened only for myself. If I could, I would send word to Erik. Why does he have to go to Vaasa so often and leave me in this house? You always feel uneasy here, as if you were in the wrong room.

Now Henrik comes out from the large room that the Old Mistress insists we all call the drawing room. He walks into the hall, boots creaking. My feet seem to move, although I am rooted to the spot. The front door opens and closes. I hear men's voices from the yard. I am sure that the Farmhand too is afraid of Henrik. A man's fear of a man must be different from a woman's. Probably it is colder, like water newly drawn from a well compared with water that has long been standing in a jug.

'Is he outside?' the Old Mistress asks behind my back.

The one good thing about this house is that sooner or later you learn not to start. 'He went out just now.'

'Where's the Farmhand?'

'In the yard. They were talking out there.'

'Did you hear what they were saying?'

'No.'

In her own room she always moves heavily, but elsewhere in the house she is quiet; the pantry door seems to creak open by itself. 'Right. You shouldn't listen to men.'

I know full well that not all of the bottles are in the drawing room. They have been hidden all over the house. She wanders between them during the day as if she were dutifully following a set path. And yet she no longer hides it, at least not from me, not any more. She has tired of concealment a little like I have tired of drawing a comb fifty times through my hair every night, or washing between my legs. When things grow useless, you let them go.

'You want some?'

'Is it the strong stuff?'

A knock, as glass hits the table. 'No.'

'I'll have a small one. Although my hands are covered in dough.'

'No matter.'

When I turn round, she pours the drink into two small glasses. The sound is like a frog diving. I sit down opposite her. She looks at me between the eyes, drowsily benign yet vacant. This tells me that today, everything's different. I wait until she has raised her glass to her lips before I wet my own with the revolting liquor. I taste what she is tasting. For a moment I have her mouth, old, doughy and sour.

'Would you like to go on a trip to Turku?' she asks.

I am so surprised that I am nearly lost for words. 'Turku? Me?'

'Yes. I don't suppose you've ever been there.'

'I haven't. Vaasa, yes, but Turku, never.'

'Good. In that case, you need to pay it a visit. Of course, there are more magnificent towns in the world, but you've not seen it and I'd like to see it again.' She rests her elbows on the table and leans her pale cheek against her palm, through which her voice now speaks: 'It's been a long time since I went to that town. It was before Arvid became sick. You were just a little girl then.'

I do not know what to say, so I say nothing.

'I should never have left. That wasn't the plan. We had a beautiful apartment and neat servants and a real piano in the drawing room. I played it when we had visitors.'

Her voice has softened and her eyes have gone behind a misty curtain. She shakes herself free and states, 'But then I had to come here to tend pigs and chickens.'

'And cows,' I say.

She stares at me for a moment and nods. 'And cows.'

'Although we have a milkmaid.'

'A milkmaid is no match for a piano.'

She is the same and yet she is not. Generally she radiates irritation even when she is trying to be friendly, but not now. She is afraid too, then. I feel the fear trying stealthily to bind us closer together. I lean further back on the bench and say, 'It's not good that Henrik's here.'

'No, it's not good. Maybe a mother shouldn't say such things about her son, but it's not good.'

'What's going to happen?'

Her eyes change again. A moment ago, they were shaded. Now they darken, open out in the middle, become tiny black abysses which suck in the gaze. She raises her glass quickly, tips it empty and says, 'I should go and feed the chickens.'

HENRIK

The new maid is sweeping the drawing-room floor. That dress is just asking my hand to slip underneath it. But servants and their betters should not consort with each other, not even when a man is feeling so weak or so desperate that both his reason and his pride – the same thing, basically – are compromised. She reminds me of someone, maybe that girl in those filthy quarters in Stockholm, where I had to struggle from one day to the next just to keep the shirt on my back. The days began grey and ended up black, if they ended at all and did not merely bleed miserably into each other. I do not wish to reminiscence.

'You're keeping the place tidy, I see,' I say.

The girl twists round, stoat-like, lowers her gaze upon seeing me and lets out a sweet little giggle. 'I can do that much.'

'That's the spirit. You should never do more than you can. It may even be better to stay a touch below the level of your maximum ability. You should never throw your ability out of the window. Someone could come and steal it.'

She stares at me stupidly with her mouth open. She shifts on her feet and licks her lips as if somebody had left honey on them in the heat of fornication. Her broad face, high cheekbones and slit-like eyes remind me of those Mongolians one saw in the streets of St Petersburg. The dress is worn but nevertheless neat and a little too tight, suitably. It is probably one of Anna's old garments. She will no longer need it, now that she is blessed with a share in a prosperous house. I bet the girl has been recruited from the village and not from Vaasa, because we all know that rural servants are satisfied with less than hired hands from towns. Financially, they are a more sensible alternative.

'Is this house a good place for a maid, then?' I ask.

'Yes, sir,' she whimpers.

'Not too much work?'

'Not at all.'

I nod as I leave. 'As I suspected.'

I take another look at her from the doorway. She is supple and light, already endowed with curves. The passage of young flesh, unaware of its future decline. Outside I naturally bump into the Farmhand, for I am used to running into bad luck. He is on his way from the shed with an armful of firewood, bare-handed and bare-headed. He must keep his shack warmer than the Russians do their saunas. He scowls at me sideways, trying to get past me, but he stops when I say, 'You were planning to heat up your cabin.'

He is ready with his reply: 'I won't need such heavy blankets then.'

'That's handy. Particularly when you don't need to get logs from your own forest, which would presuppose that you've got a forest of your own. Where have the labourers got to?'

'The place we've just been talking about.'

He does make me think for a moment. 'The forest?'

'That's right. They're felling trees, though it isn't their forest either.'

'You didn't think to go with them, as driver?'

'I would have, but esteemed visitors arrived at the house. I was asked to stay put on their account.'

May the Devil take him. A parasite like him ought to be flogged on the church hill every Sabbath. The only problem is that he would probably somehow use the flogging as a means of obtaining a martyr's crown. It is best to ignore him. I believe he ignores me, too.

I am walking along a familiar road. I once thought it safe. I did not know that it led to a dirty world. The spruce copse has become denser, they have been working on a new fence, there are no signs of war here. The air is getting cold, it eats into the skin. But this is nothing compared with the horrific winters of St Petersburg. In summer, swarms of mosquitoes, and in winter, freezing cold. That city is only a good place to live if you own a palace and a flock of lackeys who will carry logs to tiled stoves in rows of three. And yet I would go back there if I could. Not in order to be there, but in order to be far away from elsewhere.

There is my fence. It is beginning to rot, little by little. Futile, like everything I have ever done. If it is true that, after his death, a man is remembered by his achievements, I might as well refrain from kicking the bucket, because any memory of me will just spill out and trickle away. Anyway, Jansson does not need any fencing round his land. His cows have always been so inexplicably timid they are not able to muster enough courage for even a small escapade. They just stand in the safest corner of the cow enclosure staring vacantly at the house. Unless he has got a new breed, but I do not think so. All his time must go on breeding misunderstood horses and treacherous daughters.

I take the long way round, behind the lea, in order to approach the house undetected. My boots sink in the snow, I begin to grow breathless. The barn is larger than the house, but then it holds a cowshed, a stable and a feed store. Good planning on the part of one of Jansson's ancestors, who may well have been a busy man of honour. He can hardly have known he would be guilty of the embarrassing crime of being responsible for the birth of the future Jansson.

I peer round the corner. There is no one in the yard. I stand still and listen. All I can hear is the faint snuffling of cows carrying through the wall. You would expect someone to be cleaning up the cowshed or bringing fodder for the cows to chew on. Perhaps it is meal-time. I open the door a little and slink into the dim light of the feed store. I wait for my eyes to get used to the poor light.

Just as I thought. A whole mountain of dry hay.

THE OLD MISTRESS

I have to tell him. Perhaps then he will understand that he must leave. After all, the thought of money brought him back here: that cursed dream of riches which draws people to itself like those devices called, if I remember rightly, magnets. Erik can choose the right moment to tell Anna and Mauri. I will tell the Farmhand on one of those nights.

It is a defeat, of course, but I got used to the idea of defeat a long time ago. People regard me as proud and quarrelsome. How little they know me. No doubt tongues will wag. Joy at my misfortune will bring blood to those fleshy peasant cheeks, but what of it?

I will take out my better suitcases and pack my future in them.

Luckily, I have a sister in Turku and not in another backward village, where the greatest social events of the year are the littering of Gunnarsson's sow, or the butcher's hands, well used to meat, straying below corset level as he dances with the sexton's daughter. Only, the sexton's daughter has never even seen a corset and neither have any other of the fine young ladies of the district.

I will carry a parasol, sit in the park on beautiful summer days, walk along the bank of a river. What a relief, after all these years. Who knows, one day, an ageing but not decrepit gentleman may come along. He will have a sense of propriety, but the blood will still run warm in his veins and he will have the daring to let it to heat up at carefully chosen moments. He may wish to extend a gloved hand to me and help me embark a hire carriage. Then he will take me on an excursion to a remote riverside folly, a place where faded dreams can flower once more.

But first I have to feed the chickens.

THE FARMHAND

If Jansson had kept his word, many a misfortune would have been avoided. The war would still have been waged; the King of Sweden and the Emperor of Russia would hardly have changed their plans because of Henrik and the horse. In this house, however, everything would have been different.

For Henrik never got the horse. Jansson had second thoughts and paid cash for the five years' toil. I do not know to this day whether Jansson's act sprang from treachery or stupidity, or whether he wanted to spare Henrik from becoming a slave to the horse out of the goodness of his heart. In any case, Jansson's decision showed how little understanding of human nature he had. Otherwise, he would have seen Henrik not as his voluntary labourer, but as the independent man the horse had by then made out of the boy.

For a few days, we hardly saw Henrik and he barely said a word to anyone. There was something proud and dangerously mature about him as he moved around the edges of the farmyard, quiet and cold. His eyes, staring sullenly, were like coals in the wax of his hardened face. One night I woke up with a sense that something would happen. Although I heard nothing, I went out and crept into the stable. There they slept, the horse and Henrik: a primitive creature emitting a stench of dark graveyard and, against it, a tall, thin human figure. Not two beings, but one, or rather one and a half, or at least one and a third. A man-horse.

The next morning, Jansson got a surprise. He found the money he had given Henrik on his kitchen table. For a few days there was no word of the runaways. Then both returned – not at the same time, but painfully and shamefully separated from each other, like a man brought home without the lower part of his body. They were accompanied by Crown soldiers. Henrik had been caught somewhere south of Vaasa, attempting to steal turnips from a field at night. What a miserable fate for a young man: to get away with stealing a horse only to be caught pinching turnips.

Whatever we think of Jansson, Henrik escaped the house of correction on account of the farmer's mercy. Perhaps Jansson felt sorry for Henrik's sick father, and after Arvid had died of his illness, he probably did not want to stir up old trouble.

Fool that I am, I thought that with time Henrik would also forget, but he did not. In certain matters, one ought to seek the advice of women first, for they have been given a third or fourth or even fifth sight, which sees and understands many things men fail to know. By chance, I turned to the Old Mistress when I happened to pay a quick visit to the chicken shed and found her there feeding her feathered flock.

I cleared my throat, as required by good manners, and she turned and smiled. 'The chickens are laying well,' she said.

'Let's be grateful we don't need to worry about them,' I replied. 'What I mean is, there are enough causes for worry in a human's life.'

She nodded and her smile faded. 'True. Mankind seems to be made for worrying.'

'Anything in particular?'

'Henrik has been given the nature he has,' she said. She had forgotten the chickens, although one was pecking at her shoe. 'He not only bears a grudge, he has to be cunning, too. Can it be healthy for a young man to have too good a memory and too sharp a brain?'

'Is he still after that horse?'

'Yes. He's hatched a plot to get revenge on Jansson. Since Jansson took his horse, he'll take Jansson's daughter.'

I was surprised, and at once grew fearful, but I did not show it. 'Which of them? The pretty girl?'

'Yes. Anna's her name. Although, who knows, she might turn out to be a good daughter-in-law. Revenge just doesn't seem the right reason for taking a wife. In any case, the poor girl won't make up for the horse. Though you can ride a wife, of course.'

I sensed misfortune approaching, mocking and inevitable. But I did not let this intimation creep into my voice. 'It's gone as far as that? Has the day been fixed?'

The Old Mistress shook her head glumly. 'Anna doesn't even know yet that she's to be Henrik's wife. Just as Henrik doesn't yet know that I know. But I do know my son; Anna won't have any say in the matter, once it's been decided. Jansson will put up a fight for a time, but a daughter is every man's weak point. And Jansson owes Henrik, in a way.'

'I see. So he'll swap the horse for the daughter? Looks as if it's time to order wedding shoes from the shoemaker.'

'Have Arvid's old ones.'

'Thanks all the same, but I won't go to a wedding in a dead man's shoes. Could be a bad omen for the marriage. Although maybe you can't ruin a union with shoes if hooves have got there first.'

We all see others in our own way. Henrik claims that I am in the habit of skulking and eavesdropping. True enough, I happen to overhear all sorts of things, but a quiet person hears a great deal that he would rather not hear. Sometimes there seems to be nowhere in the world human voices don't reach.

It was an autumn day. Despite the chilly weather, I was lying on my back in the grass at the edge of the forest, when I heard two voices coming nearer, one clear and girlish, the other lower, a male voice not yet broken by age. I should of course have raised my head from the tussock as a warning. They stopped painfully close to me and instantly I had already heard too much.

'What if he kills you?' Anna asked, in a childishly tremulous voice. 'Father said you ought to take his knife away. They say he'd be best off in the King's army.'

Erik laughed, or at least he tried to. 'Don't worry. He's not that mad. I'm his brother, after all, and he wouldn't do such a thing to Mother.'

'Still, I'm scared. Given he's got a grudge against my family.'

'Because of the horse? Yes, I expect so. But he hasn't got a grudge against *me* about it.'

'Father still feels so guilty he can't sleep at nights. Now he would give away as many as *three* horses for free, so he says.'

'Tell your father not to worry. Or I'll tell him myself.'

Anna's voice became fluttery with fear. 'What if we were to go away?'

'Ah, so we should run away, should we? Don't. It'll be all right, I'll talk to Henrik. I don't think he even wants to get married, really. It's just tradition for the elder son to bring a daughter-in-law into the house. Henrik said once...'

I could hear their rabbit hearts beat with expectation. 'What? What did he say?'

'He said that we came into this world in the wrong order. That he's not comfortable here and doesn't want to remain here, that he wants to see the world. I need a wife, not Henrik.'

Their voices suddenly softened. Erik was probably already picturing himself blowing out the night candle.

'And I a husband,' said Anna. 'We are sure to have a good life, aren't we? Say that it is so, Erik.'

'Of course we will.'

'And children. Won't we?'

'A brood of such magnitude that we'll have to extend the house.'

But they never had children. However, you hardly feel like lamenting their fate when you compare it to Henrik's lot. Not many men are so assaulted by a foul wind that they are first robbed of a horse and then of a wife. And if the man has been cheated of the horse by his nearest neighbour and of the wife by his own brother, he can hardly be blamed for wanting to take his sorrows and his losses elsewhere.

First Henrik went to Vaasa. We did not hear from him for a long time. We got used to his absence. I believe each of us reminisced about him as briefly as possible. We let the memory come and then wiped it away. I thought of him as if he were a tree that had once stood in the yard, a tree that had swayed during storms, right by an outhouse, and had finally been felled. So I was surprised when one day a cart drawn by a healthy-looking mare appeared in the yard, with Henrik sitting on it. He was wearing good clothes, but was otherwise unchanged: stiff-backed, bone-faced, despising everyone and everything. The reason for his visit never became clear and he did not stay long. Early one morning, two or three days later, cart and mare were gone. He did not leave without a trace, however. For weeks afterwards, a mysterious, gloomy atmosphere drifted about the house and its surrounds, like the smell after a wake.

Later, we learnt in a roundabout way that he had moved to Turku. When he again appeared in the village, he was wearing gentleman's clothing and driving a two-seater gig pulled by a muscular gelding. As if that were not enough of a shock, he was sharing his conveyance with a woman whose greatest, perhaps only, talent was occasionally to burst into screeching, ear-splitting laughter. I suppose I was not alone in feeling grateful to God when Henrik took the woman and her screeching away so quickly. That week, I gave more than usual to the Sunday collection.

I would no longer let myself be deceived by the passing of time. I was prepared when one day a splendid carriage appeared in the yard, drawn by two full-blooded stallions. A real Swedish mademoiselle stepped out. And I was not particularly surprised that this time there was a weary, vacant look in Henrik's eyes. Time had clearly caught up with him. He had tried to stay ahead of it by rushing from one town to another, but though his simple cart had transformed into a carriage and screeching prostitutes had become bourgeois ladies from Stockholm, time had at last got the better of him and disclosed to him the permanence of his destiny, its inexorability: he was still the same man who had first been cheated of a horse and then of a woman.

After that, more than two years went by before we heard he was living in St Petersburg.

I should have guessed a war was coming.

A year later, it was here.

ANNA

They think I do not know. But what they do not know is that I can see in the dark, like an owl. At night, when time curls up in a ball, I see people and things as they really are. Then I open my mouth and my voice roars, silent but terrible.

Then I begin sweating and my hands are forced to console me.

Now the Old Mistress wants me to go to Turku with her. That means she wants me as far away as possible from Vaasa. Perhaps a mother's duty is to cover up her sons' deceptions, to protect and look after them. I doubt I would go that far for the sake of my own children, but a woman might change once she has borne life. I cannot know and probably I will never know. I am an object of pity as a result, but the more I think about the matter, the more it feels like a release.

I do not care what sort of woman Erik has in town. Let her be a bourgeois lady or a slum-dwelling washerwoman. Let her have ample breasts and the secret places that drive men mad. I sit here and think the woman out of existence. I take that faceless figure and crush it until the skin begins to split. Soon I will chop up that sinful flesh. I should be preparing a meal but there is still time. I stop time, it is a clock inside me, it is mine.

I hear sounds from outside. I stand up and go to the window. The cart stands in front of the stable. The old gelding is hanging its head, exhausted after the long journey. They are home.

ERIK

I do not want to look at the house. I thought I would be able to resolve the matter, but no. I let Mauri hold the reins and direct my gaze beyond the field, where no buildings are in sight. I am irked by my visit to the Crown Bailiff. A waste of time. Old Pig-Face was more interested in cleaning his pipe than in my calamity. Or maybe he is weighed down by worry, fearing that the

Emperor will discontinue his office. Never mind. Now they may come any day, perhaps as early as today. I cannot look at the house.

We come into the yard and I look at the house. The southern wall is beginning to rot and the roof wants repairing. It is no longer my concern. In my folly I imagined that, according to some law of nature, a man cannot suffer bad luck time after time. I thought: you can set a trap in the woods and go and check it for weeks and weeks, and find nothing. Then finally one day you find in it your thrashing prey.

Maybe I should have had a number of traps instead of relying on one. But no need to dwell. Now I have to bear the consequences.

Although I do have the musket in the hayloft.

I jump off the cart and see the Farmhand coming round the stable corner. I do not wish to talk to him, him of all people. He is too sympathetic. I should be whipped. Open up my veins and let me drink my own blood! But the Farmhand gives his lopsided smile, as always, and says, 'You made it to town, then.'

'I had business there.'

'Who'd go there otherwise?' He does not stop smirking. I know from his face that something is wrong. 'Though as things stand, I might leave for town even with no business to deal with.'

'That so? What's going on here, then?'

He spits sideways and begins eyeing the open field. 'There's nothing going on here, at least not yet. Or there is, but I don't yet know what it is.'

'Am I supposed to make something of that?'

I hear the front door behind me. The Farmhand shakes his head, alert, and looks over my shoulder in that direction. I turn round. My lungs empty. Henrik. He stands on the steps, looking at me. He drops down to a lower step. Henrik. Curse this day! I should have stayed in town. He pulled off a surprise, all right. He sent that letter of his. He fought in the Emperor's army and is proud of it. I did not take it as a warning, I thought it was arrogance. He walks towards me. Henrik.

'You came to visit,' I say.

He takes his time replying. 'Depends how you see it. To visit or to stay.'

'St Petersburg wasn't up to much, then?'

'Some of us can't stand being in one place for too long.'

'We know. You went on a long trip, anyway.'

Those hard, lidless eyes of his. He still thinks he can use them to drill all courage out of a person. If I were another kind of man, I would gouge them out of his head, though he is my brother. But he would probably scare folk to death with his sockets alone.

'I happened to hear in the village,' the Farmhand suddenly says, 'that if someone has run away from the Emperor's army and if that someone happens to be wise, he hides away in some backwater.'

Henrik turns to stare at him and says, in a voice that tells me his grey eyes have blackened, 'What's that got to do with anything?'

'Just sprang to mind,' the Farmhand replies. 'I've heard of such men.'

'Such men should have sought an honourable discharge,' Henrik says. 'I can tell them how it's done.'

The Farmhand nods. 'I'm sure you can. But someone mentioned another thing: that some men have had experience of being cheated of an animal and then of another, a mare the second time round, and that such men should consider...'

'What mare?' Henrik interrupts. He stands stock still, dangerously relaxed, his hands by the side of his thighs, and scorches the Farmhand with his gaze. Only now do I discern Mauri, small, shivering and frail, near the stable wall. I had all but forgotten him. Henrik turns to me. 'Is there not an almshouse in the village? Be a good place for old folk who have lost their wits.'

'I expect there's an almshouse,' I say, 'but I don't happen to know anyone who should be carted there.'

Instantly, Henrik smiles his rare, long-toothed smile. 'Is that the word of the master?'

'The word of the master of this house, at least.'

The grin freezes on his face. 'Very well. But perhaps we'd better go indoors to talk. As long as you keep that ancient lunatic away from me.'

'I don't normally need to be kept away from anybody,' the Farmhand says calmly. 'I suffer from a malady that keeps me away without being restrained.'

Henrik snorts and starts towards the step. I have never heard the Farmhand whistling before. The action carves deep holes into his already sunken face.

Mauri lurks close to the stable wall, not moving. He is sucked into the wall as if he has been left there by mistake. The shadows of the forest edge creep towards the field, and yet the sky is a single smoky cloud. I thought I would resolve the matter, I really did. But I bloody well did not.

OLD MISTRESS

I have kept his clothes in chests; I do not know why. It is certainly not for sentimental reasons. Living with a man could be compared to sharing your home with a dog or a pig, or a creature from another country – a monkey, say. Any one of those could grow dearer to your heart than a man. Not that I hated him. I could not be bothered, I lacked the energy, and to be fair, he never came into the house in muddy boots.

If I had stooped to hatred, I suppose I should have hated my father. Admittedly, the only cause for hatred he gave was his miserable failure. And he hardly set out to run his affairs into the ground, to the point where he had to marry his daughters off in a hurry; otherwise, he would have had to include them in his firm's list of losses, along with the other unpaid debts. And I could not even take malicious pleasure in the fact that my older sister was more or less forced to marry her short-sighted accountant. She, at least, was able to stay in Turku. My destiny, on the other hand, turned out to be a man who surfaced from the back of beyond. He was a relative of one of Father's business acquaintances, and prepared to make certain financial sacrifices in order to acquire a particular item to take home with him. In his far-flung native district, they called this item not 'the lady of the house' but 'the housekeeper'.

I took little notice of him at the beginning, when he began to frequent the soirées we held at our house; he was a taciturn outsider, sitting on the periphery of the company, laughing hoarsely at all the witticisms later than everyone else. One evening, however, when all the other guests had departed, I noticed to my horror that my parents had left me alone in the drawing room with this odd stranger.

I could put up with all his quirks, apart from the way he fiddled incessantly with his waistcoat buttons. This action drew my gaze to his long, crooked fingers and aroused unclean thoughts. His dark, shining eyes, which all the time moved about uncertainly, posed further difficulties, and to me he seemed near-decrepit. All the same, good manners required that I listen to him. When I did so, I woke up to find myself staring deeply into a black abyss. I understood that a decision had already been made and that this conversation was nothing but a formality. I bitterly regretted having learnt to swim, in defiance of the conventions governing girls in our circle. I could not even usefully throw myself into a river.

'It's the biggest house in the area,' Arvid said in his gruff, muted voice. He did not speak with any pride, he merely stated the fact coldly. He was peering at a space somewhere between my feet and the wall. 'And it's not far from Vaasa. And you can visit the capital, too.'

'So it's in the country,' I said. My voice could have come out of the pocket of his much-abused waistcoat. 'I suppose you have domestic animals.'

'Domestic animals?' he repeated. He looked baffled for a moment. 'Aha, you mean cattle. Yes, we've got cattle and fields. As I said, it's the biggest farm in the village.'

I tried desperately to think of something sensible to ask. 'Will I have to milk cows, then?'

He appeared determined to pluck a button off his waistcoat. 'No need. There are maids for all that.'

'Do you have dances?'

A rivulet of perspiration appeared on his forehead and set off on a journey towards one of his bushy, near-black eyebrows. 'Of course there are dances. In summer in particular, we have fêtes. A really big fête at Midsummer, and dances at weddings, of course.'

We were quiet for a while, I chewing my tongue secretly, he staring tenaciously at a space where I saw only the toe of my shoe, sticking out from under the hem of my dress, and floorboards, and a smattering of dust the maid must have missed. Then he sat up straight, left his buttons in peace and began looking at me with the same expression I had once seen on a shaggy male dog in the street, just before it mounted a passing bitch.

'I can buy a new carriage,' he said. 'A real carriage with a canopy.'

'And a piano?'

'Of course a piano.' Relief spread across his face. 'How could I forget? It was uppermost in my mind. I must get a piano.'

I have still not seen that piano. Instead, I gradually became used to this house and to people whose speech tells you they have rough palms. I did not even try to get used to the desolation of the fields and the menace of the forests, but I did find a place on the riverbank where I could sit by myself among the subdued murmur of the water and the scent of leaves decomposing in the shadow of the embankment, without hating anybody. I learnt to understand housekeeping and the significance of each of the individuals who have ended up in this household, especially that of the Farmhand, who has always been much more important than one might deduce from his station. When I began carrying Henrik in my womb, I was afraid, but I decided to cease fearing. I sensed that motherhood was terrible, perhaps sweet at times, but above all terrible. Not because one human child would be more horrendous than another, nor is it so that offspring cannot bring joy when little and be useful when grown up, but because motherhood makes it possible for future generations to be rocked by dark tragedies. On the other hand, I concluded, it could not be my fault alone. I could not be its origin. There must have been before me, maybe long ago, a woman who sinned gravely and who left her fall as a legacy to her female offspring: an Eve of her generation who had imagined she would be forced to milk cows with her fine, delicate hands.

As the years went by, the boys grew and Arvid became so sickly and so bent that he began to resemble a big-boned bird pecking at the ground. I took up the habit of moving all the yesterdays and tomorrows discreetly to one side. I have never deceived myself in this respect: I gulp down spirits like a sailor. I have done it so skilfully, however, that I have not had to compromise on my dignity, if impeccable manners are enough for that. What else could I have done, when my closest companions for a large part of my life have been empty moments and sleepless nights that end in pale dawns? I might as well have been trapped on a remote island: a pitifully ageing white woman, the soiled widow of a pioneer, surrounded by dirty natives, grubbing pigs and tumbling, whooping bugs.

I have had my chickens, and for a time I was able to watch the boys grow up with at least distant pride. But boys are fated to grow into men, and a mother has to follow this tragedy as a silent bystander. And now it seems they will kill each other, and then this, too, can be added to my never-ending list of losses.

I know now what I will do with the musty clothes in the chests. I will ask the Farmhand to build a bonfire.

ERIK

Anna will hardly even look at me. Her hips escape my hands. Her hair keeps back its scent. If I speak to her, she replies to the nearest saucepan. Does she already know? Has Mother gone and told her, after all? Should she not offer me support, particularly now that Henrik has turned up at the house, as if we did not have enough misfortunes? I feel as though, after two days' absence from home, I have lost my wife.

HENRIK

This house is a cadaver. The others are too close to see it, but it has already begun to decompose. I flinch from its decay. It is as if a collection of bones had been unearthed and dressed up in fine clothing to create the illusion of a real body. The wallpaper and chandeliers make no difference. Anyone who is even slightly in the know can scent at a ten-verst distance that the ceiling is leaking, the ridge beams are rotting and the drawing-room floorboards are as bent as an old jetty.

Fortunately, I did not come here because of the house.

On the other hand, I would rather live here than in that windowless hole in a backstreet of St Petersburg. Reeking of cabbage, the building was so labyrinthine, so full of narrow passages and steep stairways, that I often had trouble finding my room. As I searched, I would have to pass doorless nooks whose occupants would put their whole miserable lives on show, without a trace of shame. In one opening, you would see a couple copulating wildly, in another, a man emptying his bowels into a wooden tub. Then there were the rats, and the pigeons that nested in every cranny of the façade, producing the slippery sludge that coated the entire front of the house and the steps leading up to it.

The place was fine if you wanted to forget. You just needed to learn the art of forgetting to begin with. I tried with vodka. The memories failed to dissolve, though; they simply went into hiding to await the soot-coloured mornings. I tried with cheap women, but that did not help, either; I was merely left with the taste of ashes in my mouth. Finally, I could resort only to loneliness, echoey with emptiness. That lasted a while, but then grew unbearably familiar. I was too glued onto myself, I was twitching in my hole to get rid of myself. Eventually, I enlisted in the army. I do not think I have ever done anything so desperate, but at least I received decent clothes and enough food to stop the howling in my guts.

How could I have known there would be a war? It never occurred to me that this godforsaken land would drive great rulers mad. I did not consider that even a peasant nation pays taxes and is good for cannon fodder, that its barren fields and swampy forests are as well suited to become part of the domains of kings and emperors as any wilderness or desert. Nor did I understand that wars are being waged all the time, that lines of men marching with their muskets are merely the visible culmination of constant power struggles, and that actual warfare takes place in salons lit by oil lamps in which liveried flunkeys pour expensive champagne into crystal glasses, and wasp-waisted women wave their ivory fans languidly, and gentlemen sitting amidst thick cigar smoke – heirs of noblemen knighted by Gustav I of Sweden, or offspring of the Grand Dukes of Novgorod, owners of tens of thousands of souls – realize that they suddenly hanker after a ninth city palace or a sackful of diamonds, or that their lives have simply become too monotonous. And furthermore, every man wages his own wars, small, grubby battles that may be as senseless as the rulers' troop concentrations and fire commands but that he is nevertheless condemned to fight.

That is why I am preparing for my own private little battle. With my luck, he has no saddle, but that is the least of my worries. Until night comes, I will have to keep the others on tenterhooks, let them imagine that I have turned up here to demand something.

Easy. So benevolent are human beings, they are always prepared to think the worst of others.

MAURI

He does not ask me, he does not even order me. He merely looks at me sideways, meaning: unharness the horse, take it to the stable, give it feed. This is the way I have been treated all these years. In another family, there would at least be a bit of respect for one's own flesh and blood, poor or not.

Henrik, for his part, does not even deign to see me. Even so, I am not complaining. All in all it is a stroke of luck that he happens to be here. If I had had the wits to ask for anything, that is exactly what I would have asked for. In fact, he came to mind as I was standing in front of the Town Hall, waiting for Erik. I was watching the better folk of the town pass by, idle gentlemen with young ladies on their arms, felt hats on their heads and silver-topped walking sticks in their hands. One never knows, I mused. And then it struck me that if I could get them both here, I would. I am not so concerned about the Old Mistress, for she is the only one in this family who has ever shown me any goodwill.

I do not include the Farmhand in the family. If he belonged to it, I probably would not have needed to go to all this trouble.

I have finished in the stable. I walk across the yard without seeing anyone and rap my knuckles on the door of the Farmhand's hut. I stand there for a while before he appears, looking suspicious and shading his eyes with his hand as it were a bright summer day. On seeing me, he grunts, relieved, and turns to go in without further ado. I knock the snow off my boots, follow him in and sit down on the bench. The main room is lit by the flicker of the range. A pot on the fire lets out a dark, luxurious aroma.

'You celebrating?' I ask.

'I was planning on saving it for Christmas,' the Farmhand replies. 'I didn't know this day would come first.'

'Must be chicory in there.'

'Nothing in there but the real thing. Roasted it myself and ground it just now.'

'You know how to live, all right. Like a lord.'

'You can have a cup. Just don't put it about that we live like pigs in clover round here. Or should I say like emperors. Or kings.'

He pours some of the black beverage into two cups. I warm my fingers with it, take a sniff, sip the coffee carefully. I say, 'What'll happen? Will they just go for each other, you think?'

The Farmhand's face is in shadow, but I sense his meek expression. 'Suppose you'd have nothing against that.'

'Can't say I would.'

'Just don't get accidentally caught up between them.'

'Even if I did, neither of them'd notice me.'

The Farmhand gives my words some thought and says, 'Maybe so. Long time ago I met a blind man. He said he still went on seeing what he'd last taken in with his sighted eyes. Pity the last thing he saw was a powder keg exploding.'

'You're saying they've each got a powder keg?'

'They're bound to have other things, too. But a keg for sure.'

I would love to tell him. I really would. I could almost certainly trust him; he has his notion of honour. But then there is the Old Mistress. The Farmhand might be obliged to tell her and then the brothers would find out, too, and my big moment would be spoilt. I would have let it all slip through my fingers, everything I have been gathering in my fist, artfully and for so long.

So I will not tell him yet.

'I've been wanting to ask something,' the Farmhand says.

'Ask away.'

'I was thinking of asking if anything particular happened in the war.'

A cold iron stabs my insides. 'Particular? All sorts of particular things were bound to happen. People got killed.'

'Yes, of course but I meant something else…' His hands, dimly visible in the dark, seize the pipe lying on the table and begin filling it from a leather pouch. 'See, I've got this feeling there's something you've not said.'

I feel it, here and now: cries of pain, smell of smoke, blood spurting in the air and bits of guts. I squeeze my thighs under the table and try to keep my voice calm. 'Like what?'

'You tell me. I get this sometimes – I start sensing things and then they won't leave me be. And by now I've learnt that my gut feeling's generally right. God knows why.'

'Aha. Well, I don't know what it could be.'

He is busy now lighting his long-stemmed pipe. 'Perhaps something happened that wasn't really about the war. Something just as bad or worse.'

Tall, thin pines. Heather. A hilltop. Distant shouts of command and the thunder of cannon. I am crawling among the heather, dragging the musket alongside me. Then I suddenly notice on the ridge the movement of a dark-green frock coat, almost imperceptible. 'It was all bad. And you don't want to think back on it.'

'I imagine not. Don't mind me, I'm just babbling away. When a man gets old, he starts spouting nonsense.'

I do not reply. I am trying to return from crawling, from that slope. I am trying to come back and stay back. I hear snow crunching outside. Someone is walking towards the cattle sheds. The wind is howling in the field. Light, powdery snow sticks to the window. If a real snowstorm blows up, the labourers are bound to return from the woods. A puff of smoke billows from the fireplace into the room. The Farmhand twists round to the fire, discontented.

'You've had a lot of business in town with Erik,' he says.

'Erik has. I've been the driver.'

He lets smoke dribble down his lips. 'People get suspicious. Anna especially.'

I do not understand at first. Then I see. 'It's not that. Erik's not seeing other women.'

'I didn't think he was. But something must be going on.'

'No point asking me. There's this one house he goes to, but I don't even get to go inside. Or only as far as the porch.'

'So he's kept you right out of it.'

'Yes. And I haven't stuck my nose in.'

He keeps nodding his head slowly. 'But you must have found out who lives in the house.'

'A gentleman. I don't remember the name. And there are other men, too. You hear the voices.'

'I hope they're not hatching any evil plots.'

As often, I find it hard to follow his thinking. 'Erik? What could he be plotting?'

'These are strange times. I've heard village talk. Not everyone wants to stop fighting. They're still set on God knows what – don't like the Russians.'

I nearly sigh with relief. 'I don't think Erik would get into all that. He's not that much of an idiot.'

'Maybe not. But you can get into trouble if you're curious enough to listen to idiots talk.'

'Should we say something to him?'

'Might be better to wait and see. He may yet come to his senses.'

Matters tend to diminish when the Farmhand talks about them. He is that kind of man. Even if he were on the scaffold with the noose round his neck, he would remark on the mildness of the weather. He has seen much in his time. He was even in the Pomeranian War, fighting against hussars. If you ask him about it, he says he has forgotten almost everything. I bet he could still use a gun, though, and not just for shooting rabbits.

'I'd better get going,' I say, standing up. 'Don't know whether to try and look after them or make sure I don't get under their feet.'

'Do both. Look after them from a distance,' the Farmhand advises. After I have opened the door, he adds, 'But don't learn their lesson. Rancour is a bad teacher.'

The wind blows heavy snowflakes into my face. The forest is veiled, merely its outline visible. You can only sense the iron-grey sky. Erik is standing, sheltered, on the front steps of the house. He is immobile, just blowing his hands, staring ahead. He does not seem to notice me as I walk along the edge of the yard to reach the back door. I leave my boots by the door and make my way quietly to my tiny back chamber. A bed, a chair and a small table. They were good enough to give me blinds and a miserable oil lamp. The room is cool, the stove cold. I do not know what it is like in houses of correction but probably not much better. Still, I am not complaining. Soon, if I wish, I may brick up the doorway of my room.

ANNA

I turn, ready to climb the steps leading up from the cellar, when I collide with his brooding gaze. I do not see his eyes, he is a black statue against the snow-grey light, but I sense them. I feel his fingers on my skin, on my shoulder blades. He leans against the doorpost, tall and alert. I stare at him. I step backwards and the basket falls from my hand. A turnip rolls to his feet but he does not kick it.

'Caught you,' he says.

'Don't touch me.'

He lets out a laugh: the snort of a tortured animal. 'I mean I caught you in the act.'

'What act?'

'Playing the mistress.'

I decide to push past him. The doorway is too small for the two of us and he makes way for me reluctantly. Then suddenly he grabs me, presses me against himself with one hand, pushing the other inside the neckline of my dress. His hard fingers grope my neck, my shoulders, my back. My nose is filled with his smell, the sweet scent of eau de cologne and the salty scent of sweat. I slap his face and free myself from his grip. I leap up the stone steps to yard level. Down in the depths of the cellar, he laughs his hoarse laugh.

I turn and snap down at him, 'Why did you come here? Nobody wants you.'

'Just an impulse. I thought you at least would be pleased.'

'Delighted.'

'Oh, come on. Wait a minute,' he says, his voice empty of laughter. He bends and disappears into the cellar. I breathe deeply, stare at the forest, hear the sighing trees. He reappears through the dark opening and hands the basket up to me. 'You've got a lot here, for the winter.'

'Should cover us. Can't afford any more mouths to feed.'

He climbs the stairs and then stops, a couple of steps away from me. 'Don't worry, I'm not planning to stay the whole winter. Just came to visit. It can't be that bad.'

'I suppose not. If you behave.'

'Don't I always? By the way, how's your father?'

I examine his eyes: grey, steady, mute. 'My father's well, although of course he's getting on.'

'And your siblings?'

'They've all gone their different ways. Except…'

He nods once, twice. 'Except now your eldest brother is of course the young master of the house?'

'Yes.'

'That's the usual way, isn't it? The eldest son staying on as master.' You can hardly detect the irony in his voice; it is like a butterfly's wings, or a barely perceptible movement of the skin. 'At least in respectable houses.'

'Nobody told you to leave.'

'But I wasn't asked to stay, either. Since I'm here now, perhaps I should start acting the master.'

A heavy lump begins moving in my chest, back and forth, back and forth. 'Don't even think about it. Your mother and Erik arranged everything long ago.'

'No doubt. Still, things can always be changed.'

'This thing won't change. You knew it when you left all that time ago.'

'You haven't given any thought to why I left.'

My breast is being crushed, it is crumbling from inside. 'Don't blame it on me.'

'I'm not blaming anybody. It was all pure chance.' His voice becomes lower and crawls, slithering, into my ears. 'That's what makes life so interesting, chance.

You never know what'll happen tomorrow. Just as well.'

I twist round. My feet are ahead of me, my thoughts are left behind. Snow clings to my eyes. Mauri is turning the corner to the back of the house, Erik is standing on the veranda steps. I manage to cross the yard without running. I pass Erik. He says something, but I can only hear an indistinct grunt. His twisted, restless face moves out of my sight and I pull the front door shut behind me with calm restraint.

Then I rush to the stairs and stumble up them. In our room, I throw myself onto the bed. The walls pant, the quilt quivers against my cheek. Henrik's cold fingers are still all over my back. I am no longer here. I am in that other moment, when he was at liberty to explore my flesh for the only time. I do not regret it. I did not yet know about Erik then, I was innocent. Henrik's man-smell, his stubble, his hands, like snakes rising up out of black soil at night. He was hideous, repulsive, wonderful. Fortunately, I did not allow him to throb inside me. Fortunately, I did not. And yet he remained there, throbbing even now. I squeeze the quilt. My clothes rot round me, the threads loosen, I am lying here naked. The walls crack and a hot wind whips me.

I sit on the edge of my bed. Time turns over, early morning dawned in the middle of the day. Now I should go downstairs and put the loaves in the oven. Everything falls apart and we merely continue with our chores. At least that means we will not starve to death.

A sharp knock makes me start. I breathe in sharply. 'Who's there?'

The door opens with a dry squeal and the Old Mistress appears in the doorway. She looks at me with her eyes screwed up as if she were staring in my direction from afar. The words take a while to find their way to her mouth. 'Have you spoken to Erik?'

'About what?'

Her gaze begins to wander. 'General matters.'

'We haven't had time to talk.'

'You should,' she says wanly, her eyes lost. I stare at the lines etched on her face and notice that they all curve downwards. They hang down from the temples, the corners of the eyes, the sides of the nose, like the stalks of a plant that has given up. 'He may have something to tell you.'

I stand up and go to the window. Gusts of wind disperse the falling snow, so it forms slanting trails. Smoke curls out of the chimney of the Farmhand's hut, to yield under the heavy snowflakes and spread around the shack like mist with long tongues. Desolate and beautiful. I say over my shoulder, 'I don't want to know anything about the woman.'

The Old Mistress is silent for a while. I can hear her thoughts, gnawing. I sense she turns away from the door before asking, 'What woman?'

So she has decided not to face the truth yet. The whole family is like that: treacherous and deceitful. They have been given more than most but they do not know how to appreciate it. They do not respect other people, demands for honesty, life. I often ask myself whether I, too, have become a conspirator in this house; can I be trusted any more than the other travesties of humanity hanging around here? I always conclude that I am different. It is a small crime to fail to report that one occasion, an accident involving two people that has nothing to do with anyone else.

I go down the stairs. The stove sends drowsy heat into the kitchen. I have just picked up the bread shovel from the corner when Mauri creeps out of the passage leading to the back rooms. As always, he reminds me of a whipped dog. The impression may well be enhanced by that shocking beard of his, which does not suit his round, little-boy face. It is curly, like a sheep's fleece. He looks at me from under his ever-frightened brows and says in his clear child's voice, 'I thought of having some soured milk.'

'Help yourself,'

'I will. You're baking bread again.'

'Someone's got to.'

He is clattering about in the pantry. 'It's good *you* are. Will you be making some buns, too?'

'I may well do.'

I have nothing against him. I just cannot relate to him. I cannot even see him as Henrik's and Erik's cousin, firstly because he is so different and secondly because he is treated like a servant, not a family member. I never met his parents, the late master's brother and sister-in-law, but they must have been another breed. All that is sinewy and tall in Erik and

Henrik has shrunk to short, soft and slack in Mauri. Without his beard, he could be a sickly, undernourished ten-year-old. And yet he is a man. It must pain him that he looks like an overripe embryo. And then, after his parents' death, to be taken into this house out of sheer pity, the lowest of the low for evermore: that must rankle. Now he is some kind of half-creature, half a servant, half an object of charity, and it does not occur to anyone to try and forget it.

'Any dough left over?' he asks.

I sigh. 'Look in the dough tub.'

I push the bread shovel into the corner. Mauri is scraping the tub with his dirty fingers, shoving them into his mouth. I feel the filthy nails in the flesh of my cheeks. He notices my look, hesitates and tries to think something to say. He comes up with: 'Good that Henrik was able to visit.'

I feel like laughing. 'Is that what you think? Has he not always bullied you?'

He starts blinking defensively. 'Well, who knows.'

'Not that Erik couldn't improve his treatment of you. After all, you went to war together.'

'Yes.'

'You'd think such a thing would bring men together. Being in danger.'

'Yes. But I was mainly just lagging behind.'

'You shouldn't always be so modest. You probably did something heroic out there.'

He looks astounded and starts gulping down large mouthfuls of emptiness. That awkward, silent puzzlement often strikes him. At such times, you would like nothing more than to take a handful of words and cram them into his mouth.

'I happen to know you're quite a shot,' I say. 'They say you can hit a bullseye better than any other man in these parts.'

Suddenly he changes. He appears to grow, his lips stop their twitching, his eyelids freeze into immobility and his ribcage expands, as if a creature hidden inside were trying to get out. Something happens to his pale face: he smiles. It is not a pleasant smile. Slowly, wordlessly, he turns his back on me and glides away. I stare at the empty space he has left. I feel cold.

MAURI

As usual, no one asked for my opinion. They deigned to inform me. Erik went to talk to the top army brass without saying a word to anyone about his intentions. He was absent for a couple of days. When he returned, he told me that we had been enlisted as scouts. I had difficulty following what he said. I would not have thought enlisting was as easy as that. We were standing by the corner of the chicken coop and Erik explained that the King's army required men who knew these parts. I saw his enthusiasm and pride and tried to absorb some of it, but in vain. I was scared, even before I became a soldier.

'When do we have to leave?'

'We're off tomorrow.'

'How come so soon? The Russians haven't got as far as here yet. You should've said that we haven't done the harvest and—'

'There's nothing for it, we've got to go tomorrow,' he interrupted. 'We'd better start thinking about what to take. We won't be given clothes but we'll get muskets.'

'We won't look like soldiers, then.'

'Good thing too. Won't catch the Russky's eye that way.'

The inevitable wailing and scolding of women ensued and made me long for war, in the end. Not that anyone cared about my fate, but women's tearful laments are, to my ears, almost as heart-rending as the squealing of a pig up for slaughter. Consequently, I felt a degree of relief when we set off early the following morning.

You understand nothing about war until you have experienced it. And once you have seen it, you realize that there is not much else to see in this life. Maimed bodies and horse carcasses, that's your world. The oddest thing is how you get used to war, how quickly your mind becomes indifferent. Although Erik and I were not generally on the front line, our missions were sometimes even more dangerous, but after a few weeks, I stopped being troubled by the risks. We were generally on the move at night, trying to find out what the enemy was doing. I would not have believed that a man of my years could learn not to be afraid of the forest at night, but I learnt that too. I even began to think I would not mind an eternal night. Perhaps because in the dark I did not feel like such a miserable, insignificant runt.

We reached areas unknown to us, where we were of no greater use than anyone else. We could have gone back home, but instead we went on with the others. Again, my opinion was not sought – Erik would probably have glanced back more frequently if he had been followed by a faithful dog. I began to suspect that the excursion had to have some higher purpose, that we were for some reason destined to it. I had to wait until September before the point of it all became clear to me.

The battles of Ruona and Salmi had been lost and the army was retreating towards the north. We spent the night on a hill; a river ran at its foot and you could see the Vaasa road if you craned your neck. I had difficulty getting to sleep, I was not used to sleeping at nights. It was dawn when I finally began dropping off. But suddenly I heard cannon, like thunder, and muskets, banging. The noise was coming from the outposts. Erik, recumbent next to me, also woke up.

We received an order: we were to snoop on the enemy and establish their strength. So we went in a big loop behind our own troops. The boom of the cannon and the sporadic firing of the muskets became more distant as we stalked along the forest edge, crouching, alert as hunters after a timid prey. The smell of powder trailed us in the wind, early light filtered through the tree trunks like water, everything was at a standstill and unreal and too real. Erik went ahead, as always, until we turned back and again approached the sounds of battle, stopping on a gentle slope at the edge of a long field. We had a clear view. Erik kept peering through the telescope that had been lent to him by the officers. He said, 'They must be somewhere over there in the meadow, because I can see some of our men at the edge of the forest. And we're bound to see better from that hillock. We should go there.'

'But what if they're there?' I asked. 'Not too many trees on the slope.'

'Let's go carefully. If you head straight to the top and I go round to that spot over there with the three big pines, we might see them from two directions.'

'And we're supposed to count up the heads?'

'They can't really be counted, but we can make some sort of estimate.'

'Let's go, then. Got to help the King, I suppose.'

He looked at me coolly. 'Don't hurry, though. It's hardly going to help the King if we start rushing round. And he's not here himself, crawling along.'

'He may have other business to attend to,' I suggested. 'A ball or suchlike. Or some noble lady.'

He stuffed the telescope into his knapsack and some chewing tobacco into his mouth. 'Bet he's good at it, dancing. He'll know a bit about the ladies, too.'

'How do I know when you've got there?'

'I'll come to you. We'll meet at the top.'

And we did. But I had to crawl first, and I was not actually used to crawling. I was exhausted halfway up the slope, my knees and elbows were stinging, my face was all scratched by the brush. On reaching the hilltop, I came to a halt, panting. I closed my eyes and thought I might just as well stay there, rot away on the spot, end up as bones, forgotten. I did not stay there. I lifted my head cautiously and looked around. I did not see anybody.

Then I did. There was a surreptitious movement between two intertwined junipers. At the same time Erik appeared further away, bent down and carrying his musket across his breast. A man wearing the green coat of the Russian army raised himself and moved from the cover of the bushes to a massive pine, all the while staring at Erik's back. He lowered himself and then, resting on one knee, took aim. He was so close to Erik, it would be hard to miss.

I lifted my gun. I focused on the enemy. Then I saw who it was. For a moment, my heart stopped beating.

I often return to the scene in my mind. I could so easily have killed Henrik. He had never been a great shot and now, too, he took unnecessarily long to aim. Or perhaps he wanted to be absolutely certain that his bullet would pierce Erik's heart. Who knows? I do not even know how my own reaction came about. When I pulled the trigger, the decision seemed to have been made somewhere outside myself, independently of me. My actions were not dictated by my own will, but determined by a power bigger than I, unknown to me. Then everything happened fast, faster, all at once. The bullet dispatched by me hit the tree trunk. Henrik shrank back as splinters hit his eyes, Erik threw himself on his stomach and Henrik was instantly on the move, twisting sideways and diving deep into the junipers. I could see from the swaying of the shrubbery that he was storming towards the southern slope of the hill. I fell first to my knees, then into a sitting position. My eyes became blurry, I felt like my limbs were falling off my body. I squeezed my eyes shut again.

'Who fired that shot?' Erik asked. 'Was it you?'

I opened my eyes. 'I had to shoot when I saw the green coat tail.'

'How did he fare? You hit him?'

'It was all so quick I don't think I did. He ran off, in any case.'

'He may have been wounded, at least.'

'Let's hope so.'

And nothing more was said about the incident. So much else happened that there were plenty of other things to talk about. For me, the fighting ceased on that hill, in a way. We landed up in many more knotty situations afterwards, and finally in Tornio, in such wretched winter quarters that the misery is indescribable. But lying amidst dying soldiers seemed to me neither here nor there. Nothing can move a man once he has seen someone trying to kill his own brother.

THE FARMHAND

I hear footsteps coming closer from outside, along with the wind. I sit still, my elbows resting on the table, and wait. The Old Mistress treads decisively but unhurriedly, as is her wont, setting her town shoes carefully in the snow, one after the other. She stops on the steps, hesitates a moment, knocks on the door. I clear my throat and shout out, 'Couldn't afford a latch!'

A flurry of cold air comes in. The wind is shut out by the door, disappointed. The floor creaks and the Old Mistress says, 'You're just sitting here.'

'Don't I usually sit here?'

'Where else? I suppose each of us has his place.'

She sits down on the bench. My nose twitches with the familiar waft of powder. I stand up and feed the fire with a couple of logs. I get the spirits jug out of the cupboard and two cups. I pour. She watches my actions benignly, her face tired. Even in dim light she looks careworn, her former bearing gone. The years have not been merciful to either of us, but there is no point in lamentations.

'I was just thinking about the war,' I say.

She lets out a melancholy laugh. 'Is it worth thinking about?'

'No, probably not. But I was thinking how you count one as your own and another as your enemy. Your allegiance is arbitrary. You happen to be in a certain place and so you're in the army of that place.'

'Henrik didn't have to enlist.'

'You can never know what makes people do what they do. And I don't know whether we came out of it well or badly. I mean, whether we lost out when we became part of the Russian Empire instead of the Kingdom of Sweden. For it may be that we would have lost anyway.'

'I hear there are some, in towns in particular, who dream of an independent Finland,' she says. She coughs after a sip of liquor. 'I receive letters from Turku. But I don't expect anyone dares say it aloud.'

Turku. She has never stopped yearning for it. It is where she came from, in a new carriage purchased by the master. She was young, voluptuous, proud, shy. Her dress was dusty from the journey. I recall her fine wrists. Next to the big-boned master she barely looked like a grown woman, but you only had to glimpse her eyes to understand that she had brought with her an unbending will. She had the patience to wait, with that will, until the man she wedded soon proved sickly and, as a consequence, unwilling or unable to manage the affairs of the house. So the town miss became mistress of a farm. At a cost. She has paid with her loneliness and with the broken veins on her cheeks. She pawned her youth such a long time ago that there is nothing left now to redeem.

'Hmm, so we could be a sovereign state,' I say. 'I've thought of sovereignty myself at times, when I've got fed up with carving sticks out of wood.' I try to catch her eyes but her eyelids droop heavily. 'Is that what makes people blessed? Haven't we been sovereign for hundreds of years, part of the sovereign Swedish realm? And now we are sovereign subjects of the Russian Emperor.'

'It's hardly the same thing,' she mutters.

'Who knows. Some of this talk is beyond me. I suppose I'm stupid, not understanding.'

She lifts her face. Her eyes let out light. 'Don't worry your head about it, it's a waste of time. You should worry about those two instead.'

'Not much I can do about them.'

A palm, still soft, descends on the back of my hand. 'What if you were to talk to them?'

'I'm the last person they'll listen to. Especially Henrik.'

'But I'm scared. I feel that anything could happen.'

'Yes. Damned horse!'

'You can't blame everything on the horse.'

'It started the whole thing. Had I but known, I'd have gone and stolen it myself. Or perhaps killed it, if I'd been able to.'

I detect a melancholy smile in her voice. 'It's still not too late.'

'Maybe not, but killing alone wouldn't do any good now. I should…'

'Kill them both?'

'Yes. But Anna doesn't deserve it.'

'Of course not. And you'd never do it.'

We sit as we often do, in silence. Perhaps we are even breathing in unison. People are welcome to their lewd fantasies about what we get up to in my cabin. In reality, we are content with the taciturnity of two people who have experienced three decades together. There is no one else round here either of us would seek out to talk to, or fail to talk to. The others all belong to a younger generation and are consequently still unaware of their sins and those of others, or else unwilling to think about them. They have not yet disrobed and said, 'Well, if You really are hanging around up there, feel free to gawp, for this is what You made me.' It will take them time to learn that a man does not choose his lies; rather, the lies choose him, and in him they collide with the lies of others, like shadows meeting in the yard that approach one another and all of a sudden melt together to form for a moment – or worse, for a long time – a single shadow, misshapen and fearsome. I get up, grab the Old Mistress's cup and pour out more liquor from the jug. The shadow of my body, cast by the fire, embraces her. She smiles.

I have barely lowered my buttocks back onto the bench when swift feet hurry to the door. It bursts open. Mauri breathes out, his voice taut with excitement, 'We've got visitors.'

THE OLD MISTRESS

The Bailiff arrives on horseback, accompanied by three soldiers. I watch them alighting from their horses in the middle of the yard. At once I get a sense of them controlling this place, owning it. The Bailiff is short and stout, ridiculous in that fur coat that reaches down to his ankles. It hangs open, probably so that you can glimpse the uniform of the new realm. I am not near enough to see his face but I remember it: arrogant eyes, low forehead, lips that always look greasy with steak. The soldiers carry rifles which they dangle from their snowy shoulders in a pose of preparedness. They look indifferent, in the manner of men used to obeying orders.

Erik appears on the steps, stares at the newcomers for a moment and descends into the yard. Anna follows him. Mauri is standing by the wall and, at that moment, everyone else comes into view as if by mutual, fateful agreement. Henrik emerges from the barn, the housemaid's face looms at the kitchen window, the milkmaid's bloated shape appears by the cowshed door. Both labourers step out of the stable, where they must have just left the mare they used in log transport. The Farmhand stops behind the soldiers and glances at me over his shoulder, as if surprised by my failure to follow him.

The wind drops and the snowflakes, sparser now, begin to float slowly downwards.

The Bailiff speaks. I cannot hear his voice, but I know from memory that his words sound like they are being squeezed out through a tangle of worms. Even from this distance I see Erik flinch. His head turns to one side, his jaw slackens. Something must be even more wrong than I had thought. I should have swallowed my pride and moved closer. Now my dignity will not let me.

Henrik, who is standing further away, suddenly lets out a thunderous roar and rushes towards Mauri. The soldiers seem to have expected it; two of them grip Henrik's arms from behind and the third walks round to face him, pointing with his bayonet. Curses and swear words pour out of Henrik's mouth and over Mauri. Mauri stands by the wall, frail and immobile, but, to all appearances, fearless. Anna has raised her hands to her throat and is staring at Mauri. The Farmhand is staring at him, too, and Erik has turned in his direction. Mauri detaches himself from the wall and heads for the stable, barely lifting his feet off the ground.

The Bailiff resumes his speech to Erik, having been briefly silenced by these events. The soldiers let go of Henrik, who tramps crossly to the steps and sits down. Anna's hands move from her throat to her face and the Farmhand has found something on the ground to kick around.

Mauri comes out of the stable carrying a musket. He says something to the labourers, who begin following him as, in that creeping way of his, he goes over to the group standing in the yard. The Bailiff turns his back on Erik, hands a sheaf of papers to Mauri and waits for one of the soldiers to hurry over and help him onto his saddle. The legal affairs of the realm are being managed by a man who cannot even mount a horse without help. He does at least succeed in getting his nag moving. I assume he will ride past me without even a glance, but at the last moment he bows his head in my direction. I am surprised by the sad expression on his swollen face. The soldiers following him on their own mounts stare ahead, uncaring, emotionless.

The labourers and Mauri, a tight, armed group, stand in front of Henrik, still seated on the steps. Only now do I notice that one of the workers is dangling an axe against his thigh and the other has grabbed a knife sticking out from his belt. Mauri looks like an armed little boy, sheltered between them. At a distance, Erik is tramping restlessly back and forth, back and forth. Anna is staring at the field with her face in her hands and the Farmhand has started towards me, trudging slowly, his head and shoulders bowed.

When he reaches me, he raises his head. I know the old scoundrel well enough to see he is about to explode with laughter.

THE CROWN BAILIFF

Just my luck, getting mixed up in this mess. I would have had to get involved sooner or later, of course, in my official capacity. But I would have dealt with the matter in the usual fashion and summoned the parties to my office. I would not have made this long journey simply to ruin a few people's lives. Not that these peasants and their plots are any concern of mine. I do feel rather sorry for the Old Mistress, though.

Cursed be the day when that Mauri person turned up to talk to me. It seemed like a perfectly ordinary day to begin with. I had enjoyed my breakfast at leisure and wished my lady wife God's grace for the day. As usual I had gone the short distance to my office by foot. Upon arriving, I noticed a lowly creature crouching on the bench. I did not think much of it. I let him wait a good while before I saw him. Experience has taught me that haste is not advisable when one is carrying out official duties. When I finally ordered that he be admitted, I did not at first look up from my papers. Instead I let him stand there in front of my desk, another trick experience has taught me. It gives all those whiners who flock to see me the chance to put their message into words. When I did look up, I saw a runt of a man eyeing me feverishly. He had an unnaturally large head. His beard was so scanty that no self-respecting burgher would think it fit for his maid's yard-broom.

He made a clumsy attempt to bow. Then, with a trembling hand, he passed over a couple of sheets of paper. He said in a shrill, womanish voice, 'I've got these certificates, see.'

I was surprised when I saw what they were. I had not expected that. He and his papers did not go together; they were at odds with each other, like a tramp strolling around in the drawing room of a mansion, or a nobleman on a dunghill holding a pitchfork. On the other hand, I have seen both in my time, so I merely nodded and put the sheets down.

'I want all this done quick,' he said.

'The matter will be settled in good time,' I replied. 'I'm sure sir understands that, given the current circumstances, the matter cannot be hurried.'

'Why not? It's all there in black and white.'

'The documents are sure to be in order, but times have changed. Has sir not noticed that we've become part of an empire? Such a change means extensive reorganization.'

He started chewing air, shocked. He masticated away, quite as if his mouth were full of tobacco. He carried on like that for a while, before asking, in a voice that was hoarse with stubbornness, 'The law's not on my side, then?'

I could have revealed to him the real situation and explained that I was not that clear about my powers and therefore not willing to take any action. I said, 'The new situation demands that I receive confirmation of the relevant sections of the law and how they are to be put into practice. And that may take time.'

'I haven't got time,' he said. 'My time was up long ago.'

I spread my hands. 'I can't do anything about that. Sir will just have to wait.'

'And is that Mr Crown Bailiff's last word?' he asked. If he could have spat bullets out of his eyes, you would have been able to see through the holes in my face. 'That I can't get justice in this matter?'

I was growing seriously irritated with him. I said, 'Sir will get justice all right. But sir shouldn't imagine that the whole realm dances to his tune. Just leave your address in the office, go home and wait till you're summoned again for a hearing.'

'And the papers?'

'They'll stay here for the forthcoming proceedings.'

'How do I know they're safe?'

I stood up, staying calm, and walked round my desk. 'The clerk will give you a certificate with the official stamp of the Empire for the papers and their contents.'

His eyes darted about wildly. 'A certificate for the certificates?'

I opened the door for him with my own hands. 'Exactly. Please go now. And wait.'

Perhaps it was at that very moment that he made up his mind not to wait. I suspected nothing. I forgot him before the day was done. Nothing in my career had prepared me for it: that raggedy dwarf turned out to be the most devious and unscrupulous crook I have ever encountered.

I do not completely dismiss the notion that higher powers intervened in my fate, punishing me for my immoral conduct. If my offence comes to light some day, despite all my precautions, I will appeal to the fact that the harlot was put in my way maliciously, as a temptation. A man who has carried out heavy official duties for decades should be judged by different standards from those applied to some dung-cart driver or ploughman. And the conclusions drawn when judging his actions should surely also differ. I undoubtedly did wrong in getting mixed up with that slattern, but there are mitigating circumstances. Unfortunately, they are unlikely to impress my lady wife.

I suppose I fell for the whore's youth. A man of a certain age knows when he is over the hill. The valley looms down below and the man grows anxious. He is moved to mourn all the chances he thinks are lost. I was unexpectedly offered such a chance. It was positively handed to me on a platter. I happened to pay a brief visit to the salon on the outskirts of the town. No one could count me among its regular clientele, but nonetheless, I occasionally found my way there in order to escape the toll exacted by my heavy workload. I thought I would just sit down for a while, drink a well-deserved glass of liqueur and maybe smoke a pipe, when an unknown woman unexpectedly joined me. She was giggling naughtily and fluttering her eyelashes. She smelt of warm thighs.

The madam of the salon came over. She whispered into my ear that there was a room upstairs that happened to be unoccupied. Somebody had left a bed in it. That bed had clean sheets. I did not think much about what I was doing. We ascended the stairs and reached the end chamber. The woman seemed to have four pairs of hands, grown for fornication, and three pairs of legs suitable for the same purpose. Then the door we had shut suddenly sprang open. She vanished from the tangle. After twisting into a sitting position I saw that creature Mauri, whom I had by now blissfully forgotten. He had two men with him. They may not have been the most esteemed gentlemen of the town, but they were nevertheless trustworthy burghers. I knew their testimony would carry weight. I rapidly assessed the situation. I realized that if their testimonies were to be supplemented by the evidence given by the scarecrow named Mauri and the harlot who was presently pulling on her dress in a corner, and if their reports all matched up, I would find it extremely hard to prove them false. So I sent the others on their way and asked the scarecrow what he wanted from me.

'There's that business I came to see you about,' he said.

'Yes, that's true,' I replied, yanking on my trousers. 'I was intending to act in the matter first thing tomorrow.'

'Thought so.'

I had no choice but to comply with his wishes. However chaotic the official machinery of the realm might be nowadays, I do not doubt but that my actions will have the force of law in this matter. I need not have a guilty conscience in that respect. On the contrary, one could argue that I have shown commendable initiative in carrying out my duties. I would now be able to forget the whole thing, along with all the other trivia I have had to deal with in my life, had I not seen the eyes of the older mistress of the house.

If only I had seen sorrow in her eyes, because what I saw was a great deal more frightening: she gazed at me with the eyes of a woman unnaturally contented with her fate.

ERIK

He has told us to leave in the morning. The Devil knows where he got the money from, unless all this time he has had a fortune buried somewhere on my land. That is unlikely, for even Beelzebub's henchmen are not endowed with such patience. Anyway, at least the land is staying in the family. Until today, I would not have believed that he could run a pigsty, let alone a large estate, but now I would not be surprised to learn he was conspiring to acquire the whole municipality.

He is good enough to let me have a mare and a cart. No doubt he expected me to burst into songs of praise. I could argue that household goods are not part of the property, but it would probably not be worth doing so; he seems to be in great favour with the Bailiff. I suppose we must be grateful that we do not have to leave in our birthday suits.

The worst of it is, I can understand him. We have not treated him well. Pride comes before a fall indeed. We are paying now, by humbling ourselves.

Who knows, maybe I will find a position in Turku and I will yet be able to lead a life with Anna that is fit for a human being. Whatever else Henrik may say, he may be right that these times require new men. Fortunately, my aunt's husband is well connected. According to Mother, he has long hobnobbed with the Russians. I just have to conceal the fact that I enlisted off my own bat to get to slaughter Russkies. The existence of documentary evidence is unlikely, unless Mauri has it under his mattress.

All in all, the more I think about this new turn of events, the more relieved I feel. Before long, I may be able to sleep at nights. Defeat came long ago; postponing its admission has only prolonged my agony. Now, finally facing up to my loss, I am freed.

ANNA

I look at Erik's sunken shoulders and I see in him an old man. Tomorrow he will look like the Farmhand. Grim thoughts will thin his hair, his lips will shrivel into dry lines, he will rub his aching loins surreptitiously. He will see the world through melancholy eyes and look away. I approach him from behind, I rest my hand on his shoulder and peer over it out of the window. The snowfall has ceased, the landscape stretches out, shivery and empty. Erik's nape is cold bone. At times I would like to bury him as if he were a child who had died at my breast.

'You didn't have a woman, after all,' I say.

'I didn't.'

'And I thought you did.'

'That's not good.'

He has said sorry this way before. I twist my other arm round his waist. He does not move. He is a tree, abandoned by a forest that has crawled off and left him behind to be battered by the winds.

'When do we have to leave, then?' I ask.

'He said we should go in the morning.'

'Can he be that cruel?'

He turns; my hold on him loosens. 'He's come to an agreement with the Bailiff. Who knows what sort of a pact they have. If we don't go voluntarily, soldiers might yet come to turf us out.'

When I see his face I understand that he is not crushed by sorrow. He is thoughtful and exhausted, but not sad. Something resembling a smile even plays round his mouth as his eyes travel the drawing room, as if he were seeing it for the last time. He says, 'Strange how some tend to cling to places and others don't feel at home anywhere.'

'How do we know that Henrik hasn't missed the place?'

His smile is cut deeper by an invisible knife. 'I didn't say anything about Henrik.'

'But you meant him.'

He tilts his head, as he does often when in a playful mood. 'What if I was talking about myself?'

'Are you saying you're suddenly dying to see the world?'

'Well, I've heard there are these women out there,' he says, and slaps me on the buttock. But instantly, his voice grows serious. 'We should start getting our belongings together. We won't take anything big; all the furniture stays here.'

'How on earth will we manage, then?'

'We will, somehow. We'll start with the small things and build up as time goes by.'

'In Turku?'

'There or elsewhere. There to start with, at least.'

He leaves the room, lightly, speedily, prepared for the days to come. I am left to soak up this feeling. Soon I will leave these hostile rooms, which I have always roamed as if in a derelict church. Perhaps I will start combing my hair fifty times again, perhaps I will learn the habits of townspeople and take to sniffing contemptuously when I recall all this. It is good we are leaving. Our departure is already within me, awaiting birth.

I will not even bother to say goodbye to Father. I can see him sitting in the kitchen, swollen with inactivity and agreeably weary of everything. He would raise his warm, listless, indifferent gaze to me and say yes before even hearing me out. He would wag a fat finger at me and say something like, 'Feel free to leave. Just don't say one word about that animal.'

MAURI

I had to wait outside at first. It was summer. The sickly-sweet scent of the lilacs floated in the shadows of the garden, and as the evening thickened into night, the birds of the dark began singing. One of the downstairs windows of the big house was open, letting out pale light and men's voices into the yard. I could hear one man's triumph and another's disappointment. I promised to keep my mouth shut but I did not yet understand how profitable silence was. I was pleased when the maid was sent to bring me ale and sustenance. I thought it would always be my lot to be thankful for crumbs from others' tables.

Come the autumn, I was allowed into the porch. I sat on an uncomfortably rickety chair, the smell of foreign tobacco wafting towards me from the drawing room, late-night carriages clanking past in the street. I tried not to look at the woman staring down at me from a painting hung between two candlesticks on the wall. I thought how grand it must be, to live in a pile like this. I myself would have loved to be a man with the money and the daring to hang naked women, breasts pendulous as sacks of flour, on the walls of a handsome villa.

Sometimes, the door leading into the drawing room was left ajar, and by craning my neck I could see them, sitting at a round table surrounded by grand furniture and busts twisted into strange positions. There were bottles and glasses on the table. The master of the house would always have his jacket off and his sleeves rolled up high on his muscular arms. The others, too, had loosened their clothing; only Erik squatted stiff and formal in his ill-fitting Sunday jacket and unstarched loose collar. He was so obviously a peasant, lost among townsmen. I believe he kept me with him for that very reason; he might have come from the country but he still had a manservant. I was sure he wouldn't tell anyone that we were related.

He behaved well and with restraint, eyeing his cards coolly and, upon winning, shrugging off the other men's congratulations. He resembled a gravedigger, or a verger in his Sunday best, who is privately mulling over a bottle he has concealed in the chapel foundations, or the tribulations of his wife, languishing in confinement, but who behaves in front of the congregation as if filled with the Holy Spirit. He barely touched a drop of liquor, merely moistened his lips with it cautiously from time to time. When he finally got up from the table at an early hour of the morning, he was in the habit of bowing clumsily to the other players and taking leave of them in such an everyday manner that he might as well have been leaving a meeting of the village society.

In winter, however, his demeanour and appearance changed. He had learnt to lose. His collar began to droop, his eyes goggled feverishly, he kept licking his lips in a tortured manner and twisting about in his chair. He no longer despised the liquor but drank it down like all the others. Often, after we had left the house, he did not want to seek out the cheap quarters where we had been in the habit of spending the night, or what was left of the night. Perhaps he felt that fleeing the town distanced him from his losses. So we sped through the moonlit landscape, ignoring the frost and the blizzard. I was chilled by the frost but a mysterious source of warmth had lit up inside me. Although I did not yet know about the future, although I had no inkling of it, I was close to bursting into a song as I held the reins in my numb hands. I felt much more than mere joy at his misfortune. I felt as if I had died and were about to be brought back to life.

He did not always lose. Sometimes he won and paid his debts in order to have the opportunity to lose again. I noticed his increasing restlessness in between the trips to town. The house with its outbuildings, the surrounding forests and fields, were no longer enough for him. He was constantly on the move, stamping hither and thither aimlessly. His face was etched with premature lines, and his eyes stared hard, as if out of the mouths of caves.

Winter turned into spring and we were given the war. Erik gambled, lost, won, lost again. The lilacs began to blossom once more. I did not know I would shortly enlist in the army when we made one more journey to town and the luxurious white-painted house that had become Erik's private Sodom. I sat in the porch, as always, and this time I understood that it was not fate kicking Erik but human inventiveness. I saw through a chink in the doorway that the other gamblers – the master with his relaxed demeanour, two porky-faced burghers and a tall man with a permanent, ghastly grin – were giving each other signals. Both Erik and I should have realized a long time ago. They were rubbing their necks, scratching their noses, or tugging at their whiskers so frequently that you would have thought they were victims of an attack by a swarm of angry fleas. Tortured by his anxiety, Erik didn't notice anything, and I lacked the courage or the will to burst into the drawing room and tell him.

As we were leaving, the master followed Erik to the steps. He did not address Erik with the same playful brotherliness he had adopted in the summer, and even into autumn. His voice took on a rough, earnest tone as he said, 'I'll give you a few weeks. After that, the matter will have to be arranged.'

'There's a war on,' Erik said. His voice wheezed, as if it were being squeezed through a narrow tube. 'It's difficult to arrange anything.'

The master gave it some thought. 'All right. Until the hostilities have ended. But not beyond that.'

So Erik was granted time by the Emperor and the King. Soon I understood that the war suited him. Of course, he did not really like war itself, but it kept him at a remove from the inevitable march of events that awaited him once battle ceased. After we had finally retreated into the miserable winter camp at Tornio, I realized that he did not miss home at all. He would rather lie around, hungry and cold, amid the stench of congealed blood and rotting flesh. When we received the order to depart, he walked the long journey virtually wordless, day after day only opening his mouth when forced to. Not until we were walking along the familiar village road did he come out with, 'Might be worth your while starting to look for work.'

'What for?' I asked.

'You just never know. Could be I'll lose the house.'

At that moment, I was too tired to think about it. I put the matter to one side. I expect I would have done so even if I had known about the letter waiting for me at home.

Once I had read it, I sat in my room for a long while without moving. You could hear the emotional voices of the womenfolk, who were mobbing Erik in another room. Meanwhile, I stared at the unpapered wall with watery eyes and tried to digest the fact that I had been liberated. I had not even known that I had an uncle living in the New World, let alone one with a fortune to leave me. The news was almost too massive to absorb, but absorb it I did. Fortunately, I had also learnt patience, for I needed it now, along with resourcefulness. First I had to invent a pretext for travelling to the capital to arrange my affairs, and then another for going to Vaasa to speak to the Crown Bailiff. I needed to be long-suffering and cunning in persuading the Bailiff to carry out his official duties, but before that, I had to pay a visit to the manor house, a Gomorrah erected for Erik's personal use but the Promised Land to me.

For once, I went there in broad daylight. It was still a handsome house by day, but a little smaller, more modest. And the proprietor, who received me in a smoking jacket, did not seem as overpowering as he had on the dark gambling nights. But he did not let me inside the house this time, instead scrutinizing me haughtily from the front door before asking, 'What do you want? Your master must have sent you because he didn't have the nerve to come himself.'

'I don't have a master,' I said. 'But if you're referring to Erik, I've come to talk about him.'

He wrinkled his nose, with its wide nostrils. 'Go ahead, then. But I haven't got all day.'

'Erik's got these IOUs? And he's pawned his house?'

His gaze sharpened. 'It's no secret as far as I'm concerned.'

'Good. I was thinking I'd buy them.'

When I saw how fast greed can follow realization in a man's eyes, I felt like slapping my thighs. 'Buy? Buy what?' he said.

'The debts, I'd like to buy the debts.'

After which I was invited in and seated in the best chair in the drawing room. That was done, no doubt, to ensure that I did not keel over onto the floor after emptying all the chalices served by the master. The offerings of liquor did not make me like the man; on the contrary, I saw through him and thought I could never stoop as low as he had, by practising deceit behind a façade of respectability. I did, however, have to compromise that principle when the Crown Bailiff unexpectedly showed little inclination to cooperate.

What I have done is not strictly in the spirit of the catechism. Never mind. Tomorrow I will be moving into the big chamber upstairs, I will address the servants and begin to delve into the finances of the house. Then I will sit in the drawing room and chew steak, so that fat drips down my chin.

I will begin to live like a lord.

THE HOUSEMAID

Mother saw him first. He was standing by the gate, staring. One night then the next. He was small, immobile, inscrutable. Mother said he would have to be chased away because he was bound to have impure intentions. I was tempted to reply that it was high time I got to know that side of life. I bit the words back, though, and then one day, when I came back from the shop, he was sitting inside and Mother had made real coffee for him. They were talking confidentially and laughing, and Mother's cheeks were red like after sauna.

I did not think much of him. That beard made me sick. I knew I could get a much more imposing man if I wanted. I had not failed to notice how the shoemaker's apprentice looked at me when I was out and about, and the tinker who moved here from the neighbouring village. But after Mother began talking about the biggest house in the village, and what it would be like to be the mistress there, something inside me melted. I did not at first understand how such a tramp could become a master, but then I saw the money. A bundle of notes lay on the kitchen table and Mother's lips trembled. Later, Mother said it was God's gracious treasure. That I understood. We had not eaten pork fat for a long time since Father's death.

Then he was allowed into my room. They say you can do that once matters have been settled. Mother gave me some scent and told me to rinse under my arms and wash down below in the tub. He began stripping off his trousers with his back towards me, and I clenched my teeth and prepared myself for the pain. I hardly felt a thing. Come morning, after he had gone, Mother rushed to my bedside and began wailing. She asked if it had hurt badly. I said I had felt a bit of a tickle. Mother laughed, clacking her teeth. I could see her cavities shining.

Then he took me to town and bought me fripperies and I was like a lady. I did not care for the gentlewoman's corset; it was suffocating, and I found it hard to undo at the back. But otherwise I liked it in town, where everything was fine and men stared at me like I was a really good heifer and where there was a place where you could sit daintily and eat lovely cream cakes. I asked him if we could not live in town instead. He said that with his money, we could run both the big house and another in town. And when he promised that I could eat cakes until I grew fat, I saw that I loved him ardently.

Then he began to coax me into it. At first I simply listened, not speaking, and he grew agitated and began harping on about it. I put him out of his misery, telling him there was no need to go on about something so simple. I promised that if I got the cakes and the houses, I would be prepared to be tickled by as many as ten men. We had done it several times by then and I had begun to like it. A roll in the hay is not bad as long as the man smells good.

So he took me to the house. There were other women there, all being ordered around by a madam with her face powdered white. And then the Bailiff arrived and I went upstairs with him. We frolicked a little and that was the end of it. Mauri was very pleased with me.

Then he sent Mother to talk to the Old Mistress of this house. I was to become a maid. It was not such a great sacrifice, I thought, especially since I knew it was temporary. Mauri told Mother what to say to the Old Mistress, and Mother did well because the old lady wanted to see me. The Old Mistress questioned and examined me; in the end I thought she would even check my teeth. I had the wits to lie and make out I could not bake. Kneading dough makes me think of men's buttocks and then I grow damp.

I was supposed to listen to what they were all saying. I heard nothing special. At night I have had to creep into Mauri's chamber except when it was that time of the month and I was left in peace for a change. And now I only need to sleep one night and I will be the Mistress. I just hope that Henrik will not let slip what we got up to in the stable not so long ago, before he heads off. Although I doubt Mauri would be cross. He does not really want me, at least not wholeheartedly and all the time. Sometimes, while toiling away with his back all covered in sweat, he forgets my name and calls me Anna.

HENRIK

I leave the drawing room and go into Father's small study. This is where he used to sit, waiting for death: patient, modest and silent, his dry mouth working thoughtfully. Everything is as it was, nothing has been removed. Dust has been allowed to amass since his burial. There are fingerprints at the edge of the writing desk. Some of them are old, themselves dusted over, other are clearly fresh. They could have been left by anyone, but they make me recall Father's gnarled hands.

I can now admit it to myself: I was afraid of those hands. Needlessly – he would not have broken a child's nail.

The drawers are locked. I could easily force them open but that's no longer necessary. This house is lost. How did the rat do it? I may yet be roused to kill him, but that does not prevent me from conceding his merits. One has to respect a man who first leads a sweet life in a nest belonging to others, a lavishly fed cuckoo chick, and then, at an opportune moment, proves to be the lawful owner not just of the nest but of the whole tree. If I do ever shove a knife into his kidneys, I will at least take my hat off to him beforehand.

Dusk sticks to the window. I was going to wait until night-time to leave, but it makes no difference now. I should go ahead with my plan, forget this place, shake it off. I just wanted to see this little corner once more. I do not know why. Perhaps I thought I would find the familiar smell of boot grease here. But I smell only dereliction and oblivion.

I hear sounds from the kitchen. There is no one in the yard. Although it is not completely dark yet, the oil lamps have been lit indoors. I go outside. To be on the safe side, I walk in the direction of the river. I climb down the bank, trampling the dry, rustling snow, and turn into the forest. I leave footprints but it cannot be helped. The wind has dropped and an overpowering silence comes out from the pines to thunder overhead. I begin hoping for some sound or other to break it – axe strokes, the scrabbling of wood grouse, even the howling of wolves. The sky has withdrawn behind a colourless cloud and the snow is vanishing among trees that match its grey hue. The forest is not as it used to be, the years have reshaped it, I have to find my way by following my instinct. I take care not to stumble on invisible roots. I begin panting, I feel the rush of blood in my ears. Am I afraid? No, but I do not wish to think about it, I just want to do it. The deed has been waiting for me patiently and I am hastening towards it. I will settle the old debt in my way and afterwards I will be far away.

I reach the edge of the field. A light glows in Jansson's windows, piercing the thickening twilight. I am close, my blood has calmed, my lungs are fresh. I crouch as I creep across the field. I feel the frozen plough marks of autumn through my boots. I reach the cover of the old underground cellar just in time; a short, stout man, probably around the same age as me, walks through the yard. Anna's brother, presumably. The Devil himself could not remember them all, their very conception is an unpardonable sin. Now the man knocks the snow off his boots on the steps, opens the front door, enters the house. Crouched, sounding out the surroundings with my senses, I speed to the door of the barn and squeeze in through the narrow opening.

I blink the darkness out of my eyes. The stench of straw stings my nostrils. I take the iron and the flint out of my pocket and feel my way with my feet towards the tall, looming stack. I bend down and start striking fire. Sparks fly into the dry hay. I drop to my knees, I blow into it. The straw is reluctant to catch fire. If only I had tinder.

The door opens behind me and a yellowish circle of light appears. I do not need to turn round to know that I have failed. I have my senseless impatience to thank for that. There have been such moments before; they form the landmarks of my journey on this earth. My destiny is to roam the world, superior in my abilities and above all in my will, but forced to concede that inferior abilities and wills again and again get to be in the right place at the right time. They have been granted a dower and they redeem it before they are widowed by the death of their opportunities. So I may as well turn round.

'Who'd have thought,' Mauri says, casually dangling a musket in front of him, 'that you'd sink this low?'

'I haven't sunk low,' I reply. 'I was trampled down long ago.'

'Maybe. But now I've got to save you, out of the goodness of my heart. I'll have to settle this with Jansson so you won't get into trouble.' He keeps turning the gun so that its barrel traces a line across my stomach. 'Because an arson attempt can mean a ball and chains.'

'It doesn't matter to me. Prison won't be much of a change. I'd probably meet pitiful scoundrels who enjoy cheating others out of their possessions.'

Jansson, who stands behind Mauri carrying a lantern, clears his throat and says in a quavery voice,

'What if we just let this go? After all, nothing's actually happened.'

Mauri does not bother even to glance at him. 'You saw what he was about to do.'

Jansson's fleshy face wobbles. 'I saw, all right.'

'And if necessary, you can mention it to the right people. I'm sure those people would keep it to themselves long enough for nobody round here to come to grief.'

Jansson's eyes start darting about anxiously. 'Yes, I...'

'Good. You can go back into the house. But leave the lantern.'

So not only is Mauri in charge of the affairs of one house, he has also been blessed with the right to lord it over the masters of neighbouring houses. I immediately feel sorry for Jansson: a repulsively fat man who whines breathlessly even when standing still and whose sad clown's face reflects the humiliating defeat of the whole of mankind. Age has begun bearing down on him. I barely recognize the man whom I once liked and who smilingly eyed me by the enclosure fence and said, 'All right, then. If you're mad enough, maybe you should be allowed to earn the hack.' Now, as he waddles to the door, his head lowered, it seems he is struck by the same memories, for he turns to look at me and says, 'I was thinking. About the horse...'

'You may go indoors!' Mauri cuts in. His voice lashes out, a snake attacking from a bush. 'I'll take care of the rest with Henrik.'

'Right.' Jansson yields and goes out, leaving the lantern by the door.

We take aim at each other, I merely with my eyes. I could risk it and try to throw myself at him. He stands legs apart, narrow shoulders raised in anticipation, restlessly swaying his wide, womanish hips. A vein bulges in the middle of his forehead like a worm and his bottom lip glistens with spit. He is a travesty of a man, a eunuch that has crawled out from the dunghill of manhood, pitiful and therefore dangerous. He is a good shot, I know, but he will soon tire of holding up the weapon.

'I've had a word with the Bailiff,' he says.

I take a step towards him. 'We gathered.'

'But I spoke of other things, too. We talked about the war.'

I take another step. 'I suppose you made out you were a great hero.'

'Not quite. But I told him about what I saw in the war. I told him about a man who nearly shot his own brother. He would have shot if I hadn't happened on the scene.'

I stand still. I am suddenly there. I am considering shooting, but I do not want to do it. I know I will not shoot. I want only to be far away from the thundering cannon. I lean against the tree trunk, I close my eyes. I decide to wait until Erik vanishes. I stand there and I do not open my eyes. Erik will go on his way and I will inevitably return to St Petersburg, to the misery and degradation that have become my inheritance, although I never asked for or wanted that, but it was nevertheless better than staying on, only to be a spectre in the habitat of my past honour. I will not open my eyes, I will not. A shot rings out and splinters fly into my face. My eyes snap open, I leap into motion. I would not have shot. For a moment I wanted to, but I dropped the thought instantly. I never shot.

My mouth is dry, but I say lightly, 'You talk a lot.'

'I do indeed. And the Bailiff and I agreed that he'll remember what I told him should anything happen to me.'

I let out a laugh. 'You've thought it all out.'

'You think of things when you've got the time. When you're cowering in a miserable pigsty, waiting for your worthy masters to deign to give orders.' He pushes his face forwards, his head trembles and he squeezes out the words from between his teeth. 'For there are people who treat their own kin like the lowest serfs.'

'So you consider the house a pigsty? And you still wanted it? You would have preferred to starve to death, I suppose?'

'Man does not live by bread alone. A man can be made hungry by not being considered equal to other men.'

'That's as may be. But you could look at it another way: there aren't many who'd take in a Tom Thumb like you. Especially one who doesn't even know any funny tricks.'

His hands began to shake. Why does he not shoot? Am I imagining it or do I really sense his smell? He probably does not secrete normal sweat in the manner of other human beings. He exudes the odour of a muddy marsh. Like a frog. That is just what he is: a toad lying in wait for insects and larvae. I feel like laughing. I do not laugh but instead step calmly past him and continue outside without further ado. He lets out a screech behind me, almost human-sounding. I do not expect to get a bullet in my back. I pull the barn door shut behind me.

I stand in the darkness. It has fallen like a blanket. Jansson is defying Mauri's orders; his face looms sallow at the corner of the building. He lumbers towards me and splutters, 'I just wanted to say, about the horse…'

I put my hand on his shoulder; he recoils. 'It's time to let it go.'

'But I never…'

'Of course you didn't. Things just happen sometimes.'

He sighs. A man can be fat and at the same time small and bent. I suppose that is how we all end up, eventually. I am the one who always leaves and who will never need to reach a destination. I will sleep one more night here, then I will pick up my knapsack and vanish. In the annals that will never get written, let it stand: this man has shed his past.

I walk along the road. The moon is about to come apart from the cloud. It shines in the sky like fat at the bottom of pan. The gleam is not enough to cast shadows, the field of darkness extends evenly. Sounds are forced to creep along the blanket of snow. Behind the ditch, spruces shake off snow of their own accord, without needing wind. I wander exhausted and empty, peaceful. But suddenly I am alert. Someone is coming towards me.

We stop at a cautious distance from each other. I cannot see Anna's face but I sense her reluctance. I would like to reassure her, to confirm that after tomorrow, she will never see me again. At the same time, something in me wants to reach out for her. The warmth of her skin remains in my fingertips, I still taste her tangled hair. After some hesitation she says, in a voice thick with deep and indelible suspicion, 'Did you see…'

I wait for a moment. 'I did. Your father seemed fine. But he doesn't choose his company too well.'

'You mean…'

'Yes. Mauri's there.'

'I'm not afraid of him.'

'You're the last person who needs to fear him.'

She strides past me, the mild steam of her breath flaring up to my face. All I would have to do is stretch out my hand, but it stays by my side, stuck fast. I listen to her moving away and kick myself into motion. I am walking here but I see myself on another road. I see myself among ragged paupers in a filthy backstreet of St Petersburg. My feet are in front of me, I begin staggering, I feel faint. Dizzy. Someone speaks, but my cheeks do not move. Someone tries to rise within me. I am being eaten from within.

What ails me? My gums are burning, my teeth are loosening. I feel blood seeping from my armpits. What ails me, so suddenly?

THE OLD MISTRESS

I will collect the eggs at dawn. Some butter would be good because it tastes nice with eggs. Everything will freeze in the frost, anyway. I am not that bothered about lard or bread. But I expect we will eat well before we set off and will not eat again until we reach Vaasa. On second thoughts, I will put on the fur hat Arvid brought me from Stockholm. A few of the eggs might remain unfrozen inside it.

ERIK

Henrik has appeared in the doorway. I do not know how long he has been standing there, silently swaying, seemingly not breathing, aiming his mute eyes at some vague spot. His hands are fists, the muscles of his face are taut. He must have come in only a moment ago, but his forehead is slick with sweat. He looks unwell: long-term sick, convalescent. He looks like a man you would see in a dream, rising up from among gravestones in a churchyard.

'We thought we'd get our things together, for the journey,' I say, pushing the drawer of the bureau shut. My eyes become fixed on Mother's tiny porcelain figures, their fragile shapes. Are they what Henrik is gaping at? 'We won't need much, from the look of it. You don't realize how little you have until you start gathering it all together.'

He keeps staring a fraction past me, as if incapable of looking at me directly. His voice sounds strange when he says, without moving his lips, 'I suppose you've got a gun?'

'I do. Or I did, at least. When I last saw it, it was in Mauri's hands.'

He shuts his eyes and bites his lips together as if trying laboriously to compress a new thought. 'What about Father's old shotgun?'

'It's with the Farmhand. Ask him.'

He opens his vacant, bottomless eyes. 'No point asking him.'

Suddenly I remember him as he once was. Once we were small boys and his eyes were not hard and hostile. His laughter, which in those days rang out often, was not distorted by mockery or contempt or suppressed rage. He was my brother then, nothing could come between us, I could trust him. He coaxed an enraged bull to abandon its attack on me. He shinned up a tree to fetch me when I did not dare to come down. It was a summer evening, mosquitoes circled above the slow, flowing, glittering surface of the river and we floated our fishing rods in the water and he said he wanted to be a fish and swim out to the sea and to foreign countries. I asked to go with him and he said I would need only to hang on to his fins. But his fins began to grow, sprouting ugly scales and pushing out spikes and forcing him into deeper waters, into a gloomy pond of kind I had no business to enter. And as if that were not enough, life threw horses and loves between us.

'What do you want with a gun?' I ask.

'I thought of going to the forest.'

'You can't see well enough to hunt now.'

'My prey is close.' He lowers his gaze, sees an answer to a silent question on the floor, nods once then twice. 'I'll go to the river, then.'

He turns and leaves and I understand. I curse, I rush after him. He is already stepping outside, the door lets in a cold blast, I stuff my feet into my boots. I stumble on the threshold, skid on the steps, hurl myself down them and after him. He is slower than I, always has been, his feet heavy as if his body were weighed down by the merciless weight of the world's sins, all collected together. I grip his shoulders and he turns, and now I see his grey eyes without seeing them, the furious glow of the rough weave of an eternal night. He swings his fist in a high arc at me and I cling to it with both hands and squash him with my full weight and he begins falling, back-first, in slow motion, a tree yielding reluctantly from its base, and lets out the broken, intensifying roar of a wounded animal, the like of which I would not have thought human lungs able to emit.

THE FARMHAND

Nature toys with humans, pokes fun at us. It is a grim game in general, as when frost hits fields, or a river floods, or a thunderbolt strikes a man dead. At times one feels as if the earth were waging a war against men, along with the sky, the winds and of course the snow. A human being puts up a fight as best he can, but he might as well throw himself down and wait for the axe to fall.

Nature is having good sport as I rush out of my cabin and the moon charges forth from behind a cloud in order to light up the absurd misfortune of man. I was just sitting by myself, listening to my own taciturnity, so I am like someone newly woken. But I trot as fast as my stiff legs will carry me. The brothers are rolling around on the ground and Erik is shouting, he's letting out a dull, almighty, unending roar. But no, the sound is not coming from Erik. It's Henrik who's shouting. Impossible, altogether contrary to the laws of nature, conclusive evidence of the imminent end of the world, the deluge, the Last Judgement. I reach them just as the Old Mistress and Anna appear on the steps. I try to get hold of either of them, of something, a hand, a neck, or a shoulder, but no grabbable limbs protrude from the ball they form, except four, or it looks like eight, legs that move so quickly that my old hands cannot catch them. They have become one unified creature and at the same time more than two men, and not just men, but two-and-two-thirds, or at least two-and-a-half, man-horses, with bared yellow teeth and furiously kicking hooves.

At that moment, a heavy figure throws itself down on top of them from my side and everything ceases. The human horse stops flailing and twitching and all you can hear is the laborious breathing of the brothers. The Old Mistress lies across them like some sort of eternal foremother, sacrificing herself for her offspring and conquering them with the sheer might of her motherhood. She is a stone statue, the first mother of the ferocious females of the past, who has plunged off her pedestal. She says calmly, as if looking up distractedly from her rocking chair, 'Stop this din!'

I reach out my hand and help her onto her feet. She leans against my shoulder, but not by any means out of exhaustion. Erik, too, is soon on his feet, while Henrik pushes himself upright bad-temperedly, moving slowly like a bear that has just crawled out of its cave. Anna finds her way quickly to Erik's side, but in the gleam of the blaspheming moon I notice that her eyes, oddly shiny and hot, are stuck on Henrik. This is not the first time I am troubled by nothing being quite what it seems.

'Why didn't you let me go?' Henrik asks threateningly.

'Because I've still got my wits about me,' Erik answers. 'And because it's the wrong way to go.'

'Who are you to decide? Should I take orders from a man who cannot even hold on to his house?'

'I may not have held on to the house but I did hold on to you.'

I see it coming: Henrik presses his shoulders forwards and his fists start swinging by the sides of his thighs like weights fastened on plumb lines. I leap between them, facing Henrik, and say, 'Why don't you go now? You can see well enough to travel in the moonlight.'

He eyes me for a moment, stunned. Then his eyes flash and he raises his hand. I wait for the blow, motionless. I will not close my eyes, I will not. He yanks his fist behind his shoulder and his face, turned towards the moonlight, twists with immense rage. I see the blow before it is on its way and I realize this could be the end.

'Stop it, Henrik!' the Old Mistress snaps in a steely voice. 'You will not hit your father!'

That is how it happens in the end. I have been waiting for this revelation for a long time, imagining a solemn affair, a little like an announcement in church or a declaration issued in the market square that people have gathered to hear in their Sunday best, pious expressions ready on their faces.

A confused, bubbling sound escapes from Anna's lips. Erik looks at me with a frozen face. Henrik stands with one hand drawn behind his shoulder, but his head droops to the side as if he has been hit in the face or the muscles in his neck have given way.

'No point pretending. You did know, or at least guessed,' the Old Mistress says coldly. 'Arvid wasn't up to making babies, even before he got ill. And don't judge me. I've got blood in my veins and, once it surges, I have a hunger that eating won't cure.'

They have always had different ways of walking, Henrik and Erik. Henrik moves slowly and heavily but Erik is still boyishly agile, one moment here, the next gone. That is why I remain stupidly still as Henrik executes a twist in the air and launches into an incredible run. He gallops along the surface of the yard, trampled down hard, in the direction of the slope leading to the river. Erik dashes off. I am still pawing snow with my feet until I finally work up some speed and jog after them as best I can. The path thuds, the moon casts fleeting shadows, snowy spruces twist and turn anxiously beside me. Now Erik is catching up with Henrik, I lag further and further behind, I stumble, I nearly fall over, damn this old age, I see Henrik reaching the riverbank down below, and the foam of the black water, flowing between the icy banks, and then Henrik, suddenly up in the air, above the river, suspended for a moment in a void. Then he falls, breaking the swirling, muscular surface of the water. Erik makes it to the embankment and I see what is about to happen just before it happens and I try to shout, pathetically and with whining lungs, 'Take your boots off!'

He does not take them off, he does not hear me, of course. Now he freezes in the air with his arms stretched out, his head pushed between them – the tautening of a slender figure, like a flexing bow – and then he too is in the water, and I carry on trotting along the sloping bank, clumsy as a hobbled cow. I adjust my route and get off the path, I turn downstream, but it is a mistake because I sink into the snow, right up to my thighs, and so I have no choice but to return to the path. My temples are thumping, my chest is about to burst and my knees threaten to give way, I start scooping air with my hands as I run and suddenly the river is there, I nearly tumble in myself but manage to turn and begin dropping down the embankment downstream. The river is strong, too strong, cunning under its soft skin, from afar I see a hand raised out of the water, but then it, too, vanishes, so death must be certain now, I carry on trotting along the riverside but only to trot towards the end. I feel like throwing myself into the river or collapsing in the snow and sinking into it and asking for forgiveness for all my sins, and roaring out a final prayer before they bury me: a prayer in my own words, one that has been waiting for me all along, dedicated to me.

HENRIK

He is finally mine, I clutch him, and I do not let go, I squeeze his hot flanks with my knees, the wild flying of his mane, his hot breath on my face, I am riding him.

She is finally mine, I clutch her, and I do not let go, I squeeze her hot flanks with my knees, the wild flying of her mane, her hot breath on my face, I am riding her.

We gallop deeper and deeper, towards darkness, together, free, swaying, now.

ERIK

Henrik. Fish fins. I bought Jansson's horse for you. I cannot give you both of them. I will get down from the tree, Henrik. I will come down.

THE FARMHAND

But just then the dark surface breaks and first one head pushes through, then another. The heads do not look as if they belong to two separate bodies, but to a two-headed creature risen out of the sludge. Erik manages to turn onto his back and tries to get to the bank, frantically splashing about with one arm while using the other to support Henrik's head. I reach them and begin looking feverishly for something I can stretch out. Among the shadows cast by the insolent moon, I spot a dry branch sticking out of the snow. I snatch it free from the suction of the lumpy snow and fling myself onto my knees by the water to hold it out to Erik.

'Grab this!' I shout. My cry sounds like wordless roaring. 'I'll pull you out!'

Erik beats the rushing water with his free hand. His head bounces on the surface, while Henrik's looks immobile, like a stone sticking out of the river. I try to extend my arms and slither over the bank until almost the whole of my upper body is swaying above a void. Erik lets out a yell – desperate or anguished or merely frantic – and rises partially out of the water, springing out of it backwards in an arched leap. Henrik's head is in his arms like a loaf clutched by a starving man.

Erik clasps the stick I am holding out. I tug with all my might, for a moment I worry that their weight will pull me into the river, but now Erik grabs my shoulder and then the embankment, and I use my last ounce of strength to lie back, tucking my feet underneath myself for grip. I reach forward to seize Henrik's wet shock of hair. He becomes detached from the river like an exhausted fish and collapses face-first on top of me.

I hear their panting through my own puffing. Henrik starts coughing water onto my face, I shift him off me. I hear sounds approaching from further along the bank. I push myself into an upright position, I sway. The brothers lie on the ground next to each other with their chests heaving, so alike. Anna reaches us and throws herself onto her knees next to Erik. The Old Mistress has stopped at the bend in the river, not because she does not have the strength to go any further, but because she can see all she needs to from where she is. I bend down to push Anna to the side and help Erik to sit up by taking hold of his armpits.

'You should've taken your boots off,' I say. 'They gulp down water.'

'There wasn't time,' he gasps.

'We've got to get into the house at once,' Anna says. 'Otherwise you'll catch your death.'

Henrik lifts his head listlessly. 'Doesn't sound like a bad idea.'

'Keep your mouth shut!' Erik snaps. 'I'm not planning to go to my grave because of you.'

'Though you nearly did,' Henrik says, his voice quivering.

Erik pushes himself up. 'I would have let go.'

'I expect you would have. But would I?'

We half-run upstream. The Old Mistress has already turned round to trudge back ahead of us. Henrik trails behind, his head bent, hugging himself with both arms. Erik turns to me and asks, 'It is true, then?'

I nod. 'It's true, most likely, no way round it.'

He thinks for a moment and states calmly, 'Why not, suits me fine.'

I look over my shoulder; Henrik is following us. He looks lonelier than ever as he comes up the slope. I stop to wait for him. This is the way he must have trudged for months, struggling uphill, sullen, alone. Reaching me, he is minded to pass at first, but then he turns his face towards me and, with it, his eyes. They lack their usual gleam. Maybe it is because of the bluish light of the moon that his expression appears almost gentle, unless he is just exhausted, unless his strength has finally been depleted and he has, at last, given in.

'St John used to baptize folk in a stream,' he says.

THE OLD MISTRESS

We had no choice in the matter. No generation can fail to hear the demands that are sung out by the choir of the tribe that came before. The legacy of landowners in particular is to burden their offspring with their gains and losses; they are to succeed, come what may. When it began to dawn on Arvid and myself during that night in the bridal chamber that he had not been blessed with the capacity to make fruitful the field that he had been given to sow, something that later became undeniable, we understood that hostile fate had picked on us and was beginning to nudge us towards shameful oblivion. I would have borne our situation, but it made the sickly Arvid seriously ill. The flesh fell off his bones, he lost his appetite, he stayed awake brooding at night. The gloom in his eyes reached such proportions that even animals shied away from him and when he took to his bed in the evenings, you would think he was arranging his limbs in a coffin.

'I'm not fit to make babies,' he sighed, resigned.

'It isn't your fault,' I tried to comfort him.

'I must have done some wrong, to be punished like this.'

'Maybe you're having to pay for the sins of past generations.'

'In that case there must have been many generations of sinners in this family. I'd happily go hang myself so you could get a new husband, but that too is a sin, as we know, and there's nothing to be gained from me roasting in hell.'

I do not remember now, or I do not want or dare to remember, which one of us came up with a way out of the horrible situation. I only recall, or choose to recall, how once again we had laid our heads on the pillows of our marital bed, airless in its chastity, and the idea worked itself into our subdued talk, as if presented by heavenly mercy. Arvid said, 'What if I had a chat with the Farmhand? We could agree on one Sunday a month.'

I thought the suggestion over. 'I wonder if once a month is enough. Wouldn't two or three times be better?'

'Let's say that, then. I can reward him with a cow.'

But the Farmhand did not care to be paid with a cow. He explained that first of all it was a matter of honour for him to help his masters in such a matter and, secondly, he did not expect the service we had agreed upon to prove altogether unpleasant. And so I started creeping into the Farmhand's small cabin at night, unbeknown to the servants; at first two or three times a month and then, emboldened, four or even five times. In the beginning, we stuck to Sundays, as planned, but despite our earnest efforts, the hoped-for result did not come about. That is when Arvid concluded that we had perhaps misinterpreted the Lord's wishes – Sunday being a day of rest, it might not be favourable for conception, and therefore we should try on weekdays too. Performing this taxing night service after a long working day put quite a strain on the Farmhand, but Arvid had a neat herb garden laid out behind the Farmhand's cottage and also forced him to accept as a gift the biggest pig that could be found in the district. As you might expect, the Farmhand resisted these luxurious gifts till the end, but I saw how he chuckled, when alone, at the surprising improvement in his living conditions.

Whatever atrocities Arvid's forefathers had committed, they were eventually forgiven: I became pregnant with Henrik. His birth was joyous, but we did not dare to trust in fate firmly enough to be satisfied with only him – many a firstborn is snatched straight from the cradle by the Grim Reaper. So I had to make my way back dutifully to the Farmhand's bed, for which Arvid had procured a soft cotton mattress from Vaasa to make me happy.

The joy brought by offspring came too late for Arvid, however; it did not make him a healthy man. He seemed to fade away gradually, from day to day, and I had to take more and more responsibility for the affairs of the house. At the same time, I became oppressed by the loneliness of the man, who would barricade himself in his cramped study. At night, I could not help thinking about my lawful spouse sitting sleepless in his worn leather chair, broken by ill health, pale and wounded, while I lay drowsy, the needs of my blood satisfied, next to the Farmhand. I knew that Arvid would not have allowed me to pity him, but I could not help doing so.

'I feel that he's approaching death. It may take weeks or years but it's coming,' I said to the Farmhand. 'So I thought that we could have a break from these services of yours. It'd feel more decent somehow.'

And so came long and quiet years, through which Arvid struggled with amazing endurance, holding on to life, and I stayed away from the Farmhand's bed. I watched my children grow up, I spent a lot of time by the river in summer and in winter remained mainly indoors, letting time crawl by. I would not say that I was hoping for Arvid's death. I anticipated it because it was inevitable. When the moment finally came – when the housemaid found him one morning, lifeless in his chair – I did not experience overwhelming grief any more than I did great relief. I felt I had encountered an inescapable given, just as I did when I first came to this remote place as Arvid's bride. I waited for as long after the funeral as I deemed fitting and then crept into the Farmhand's shack to discover that he had slept all these years on his old straw pallet, keeping the cotton mattress strictly in storage for me.

I did not become pregnant again. My blood calmed down, it was in ferment only now and then, and the agony of the long days began to trouble me. I started to shorten my days with the help of spirits. At times I paused to wonder whether I should reveal to the boys their origin, but I kept deferring the moment, carelessly and irresponsibly. I put off the future for a long time, but now it is here.

ANNA

I stand with my back against the window and watch Erik about to fall asleep. He is stretched out on the bed, his head bent tiredly to one side. A strong vein throbs at his throat and I feel its pulsing in my fingertips. I feel it on my temples, my tongue. Frozen moments always carry the salty taste of impatient skin.

I turn to glance outside. The Farmhand and Mauri are standing in the middle of the yard, which is chalked by the moonlight; Mauri seems to be explaining something fervently and the Farmhand keeps nodding, as is his habit: exaggeratedly, almost as if he were bowing and scraping. I sense the frost, polishing their words bright. The darkness in the forest yearns for their echoes. Mauri grabs the Farmhand's hand. Immediately, the spaces between my fingers seep with clammy sweat.

There is a knock on the door and the Old Mistress pushes her face in. It is a calm face; the customary numbness of the evenings has peeled off. On such an evening, then, she leaves her bottles be. She looks at me tenderly and clears her throat, meaning for Erik to open his eyes. When Erik has done so, she says, 'I think we should set off sooner rather than later.'

Erik raises his head and asks in a feeble voice, as if he were still gasping for air on the riverbank, 'By night?'

The Old Mistress nods. 'The sky's clear and you can see in the moonlight. And there are no neighbours or villagers around to gawp at us.'

'That's true,' Erik concedes. He levers himself onto the edge of the bed. 'Doesn't make any difference to me, let's leave by all means.'

'I'll go and prepare some sustenance first,' the Old Mistress says. Her head vanishes from the doorway, but reappears in no time at all to add, 'I must put some eggs in the hat.'

The head disappears again. Erik looks at me, baffled, and repeats, 'In the hat?'

I shrug. I should take something to cover my head, too. I can already see myself in the gig. The road shines ahead of us, a channel piercing the gloom of the forests. The past will be left behind in its entirety; the days to come are calling us to them. I will have to get used to a big town, the noise echoing from the streets and the unkindness of busy people, but I am still young, and eager to accustom myself. I will learn to look bored and toss my head proudly, and if the townsfolk try to boast about their knowledge, I will tell them my bloodiest tales of pig-slaughterings and tough calvings, and if that does not help, I will hint at a contagious disease I have brought with me, one I've picked up from animals. At night I will lie down next to my husband and hear the townsfolk – the listless sighing of city lungs, the exhausted twisting of city hearts – and I will turn over, pleased that I can still sense, from afar, the peace of the fields and the silence of the forests. I will be there and at the same time here; I will be in the air amidst all that is alive, I will be in myself.

'I'd better make sure the mare's been fed,' Erik says, and walks stiffly out of the room.

His steps grow faint. I hear the banging of the front door, I watch him cross the yard. Henrik comes from the opposite direction in dry clothes he has found somewhere, his shoulders still hunched as if he were cold. They exchange a few words without stopping.

Henrik nods and looks like the Farmhand, just as he is supposed to do. I stir myself and slip light-footedly into the stairway. Not all the words remain in my mouth, some drip off my chin soundlessly. I bump into Henrik in the porch. I shove him by the chest as close to the door as possible and whisper, 'Don't interfere in my life again.'

Until a short while ago his eyes were as sharp as poker points. Now they look blanched and lost; they have become the eyes of a child who has just woken up. He laughs sadly and replies, 'Why would I? I thought I might go to America.'

I glance behind me, just in case. My ears lie in ambush for sounds. 'How will you get there?'

'I might get a job on a boat. Otherwise, I'd have to earn the money first.'

'As long as you don't earn it in Turku.'

'No, I won't. Although there is a port in Turku.'

'Please, will you stay in the port?'

He contents himself with nodding. Now I have to swallow the bile rising from my stomach. A clock begins striking inside me, I am thrown by the maelstrom of time, the early morning is cool and sweaty. I resist. I grip Henrik's arm and say, 'You were good once.'

His face twitches, lowers. 'And so were you.'

'Although I knew nothing then.'

An unprecedented din comes from the direction of the kitchen; we both twist round, stunned, in that direction. The Old Mistress is singing. Henrik laughs soundlessly and looks at me with his face opening out, as if seeing me for the first time. 'But that's not why. It was…'

'Yes,' I say. I turn my back on him. 'Yes.'

THE FARMHAND

They sit in the cart, stiff and solemn. They could well be leaving for a nocturnal church service. Henrik, holding the reins, wears clothes retrieved from the late Master's estate, the Old Mistress sits next to him, and Anna and Erik are behind them with the chests and bundles. I do what I have to do: I walk to the side of the cart and look the Old Mistress in the eyes by way of a goodbye. The moonlight falls on the lines of her face, gets caught in her eyelashes and stays there, glittering.

'You're staying?' she asks, or states.

'I have no choice,' I say, 'I've been given the title of Farm Manager.'

'You think you'll get on all right?'

'With the title or the man? I've always got on with Mauri. And what can he do to me?'

She smiles. 'No one can do anything to you.'

I move over to shake hands with Anna and Erik. Anna smiles. She has wrapped a blanket round her shoulders over a thick coat and looks very young, like a little girl excitedly anticipating a journey. Erik holds my hand between both his palms and says, 'You'll come and visit us in Turku.'

'Duties permitting,' I promise. 'I have become an important official.'

'And you must write, since you have that skill.'

'Unless Mauri hires a scribe to help me out.'

I walk round the cart and stop by Henrik. He crouches, stooped, his head drawn between his shoulders, the features of his thin face sharp and stubborn in the bluish light. I have just opened my mouth when he flings the reins from his hands, jumps onto the ground and sets off determinedly past me, towards the house. He takes a lantern suspended from a pillar of the veranda and continues with a heavy tread towards the stable. He has already pulled open one half of the double doors when I go after him.

He stands by the stall, circled by the dim, flickering light of the lantern. I stop by his side. We observe it in silence: a creature that has strayed into our age from the airless centuries of the past, a creature that exudes the nasty smell of a churchyard and whose malevolent gaze bores into us from its immobile eyes, eternally judgemental and accusatory. It does not breathe, it emanates quietly, you can feel life flowing in and out, eternally, through its tough skin.

'Erik must have paid a pretty penny for Horse,' Henrik says, looking at the animal he worked so hard to win.

'On the contrary. He got it practically free as it was no good to anybody. Jansson was probably pleased just to get rid of it.'

Henrik nods. He stretches out his hand, the horse has to bend its head, swaying up there so high, to nudge the palm with its rounded muzzle. I feel the warm saliva smell of its breath. Henrik smacks his lips. The horse, or rather the horse-like being, more mysterious and more powerful than a horse, responds by throwing its head up and letting out a sound: not a neigh but rather the boom of an out-of-tune organ, or the hollow, screeching din of heavenly trombones – or infernal instruments. I step back, poised to raise my hands to my ears.

'You thought you'd let it go,' I say.

Henrik nods. 'That's what I thought.'

I walk outside and move away from the doorway. The horse steps out of the stable slowly, haughtily and insolently. It could quite easily dig man-sized holes in the ground with its hooves, but refrains out of sheer superiority. In the middle of the yard, it stops to look with scorn at the cart and its passengers. Shaking its head discontentedly, the horse carries on to the edge of the field, as if trying to forge those heavy hooves into the earth. It does not need to jump over the ditch. It simply crosses the ditch without acceleration. In the middle of the field, it hurtles into a gallop.

Subscribe

Subscribe to Peirene's series of books and receive three world-class contemporary European novellas throughout the year, delivered directly to your doorstep. You will also benefit from 40% member discount and priority booking for two people on all Peirene events.

PEIRENE'S GIFT SUBSCRIPTION
Surprise a loved one with a gift subscription. Their first book will arrive tied with a beautiful Peirene ribbon and a card with your greetings.

The perfect way for book lovers to collect all the Peirene titles.

> 'What a pleasure to receive my surprise parcel from Peirene every four months. I trust Meike to have sourced for me the most original and interesting European literature that might otherwise have escaped my attention. I love the format and look forward to having a large collection of these beautiful books. A real treat!' GERALDINE D'AMICO, DIRECTOR, JEWISH BOOK WEEK

Annual Subscription Rates
(3 books, free p&p, 40% discount on Peirene events for two people)
UK £25 EUROPE £31 REST OF WORLD £34

Peirene Press, 17 Cheverton Road, London N19 3BB
T 020 7686 1941
E subscriptions@peirenepress.com

www.peirenepress.com/shop
with secure online ordering facility

Peirene's Annual Series

Peirene carefully curates its books in annual series. Each year we publish three titles from all over Europe, linked by a common theme. These books lend themselves to comparison and give insight into trends from the European literary scene. All our authors are award-winners and/or bestsellers in their own country.

Free Peirene e-book samples can be downloaded at:
www.peirenepress.com/samples

....

PEIRENE'S SERIES OF THE FEMALE VOICE
Female protagonists and strong female narratives written by men and women. The books tell the stories of a French mother who struggles to protect her two sons from the world, of a Catalonian woman's life and loves during the Spanish Civil War, and of an hour-long walk with a pregnant young German wife in 1943 Rome.

Beside the Sea by Véronique Olmi
Translated from the French by Adriana Hunter
'A mesmerising portrait ... it should be read.' GUARDIAN

Stone in a Landslide by Maria Barbal
Translated from the Catalan by Laura McGlaughlin and Paul Mitchell
'So vibrant that is makes me want to take scissors to everything else I read.' GUARDIAN

Portrait of the Mother as a Young Woman
by Friedrich Christian Delius
Translated from the German by Jamie Bulloch
'This is a small masterpiece.' TLS

....

PEIRENE'S SERIES OF THE MAN
Male authors, male protagonists and male struggles with reality, from Germany, Holland and Austria. The books tell the stories of a man faced with the next world and the shifting sands of the

world he is in, and of a road trip with a boxer and a family man, together with a collection of Kafka-esque short stories about loss of identity in the modern world.

Next World Novella by Matthias Politycki
Translated from the German by Anthea Bell
'Inventive and deeply effecting.' INDEPENDENT

Tomorrow Pamplona by Jan van Mersbergen
Translated from the Dutch by Laura Watkinson
'An impressive work from a leading Dutch writer.' DAILY MAIL

Maybe This Time by Alois Hotschnig
Translated from the Austrian German by Tess Lewis
'It is very refreshing to be confronted by stories which so firmly refuse to yield to conventional interpretation.' GUARDIAN

....
PEIRENE'S SERIES OF THE SMALL EPIC
The novella-length books in this series present truly big stories in small packages. They include a Finnish Shakespearean drama, a Danish literary crime novel and a Swiss novel about the most influential Chinese painter of all time, Bada Shanren.

The Brothers by Asko Sahlberg
Translated from the Finnish by Emily Jeremiah and Fleur Jeremiah
'Asko Sahlberg brings regal drama to a farmhouse ... The comparison with Shakespeare might seem grandiose, but it's justified.' HELSINGIN SANOMAT

The Murder of Halland by Pia Juul
Translated from the Danish by Martin Aitken
'Just as Umberto Eco's The Name of the Rose *made crime fiction appear intellectual, so Pia Juul's* The Murder of Halland *dismantles the rules of an entire genre.'* DAGENS NYHETER

Sea of Ink by Richard Weihe
Translated from the Swiss German by Jamie Bulloch
'A powerful, poetic book. A two-hour enchantment.' KULTURSPIEGEL

Peirene

Contemporary European Literature. Thought provoking, well designed, short.

'Two-hour books to be devoured in a single sitting: literary cinema for those fatigued by film.' TLS

Online Bookshop

Subscriptions

Literary Salons

Reading Guides

Publisher's Blog

www.peirenepress.com

Follow us on twitter and Facebook @PeirenePress
Peirene Press is building a community of passionate readers.
We love to hear your comments and ideas.
Please email the publisher at: meike.ziervogel@peirenepress.com